*The Gingerbread Tales
Anthology*

The Gingerbread Tales Anthology

Justin Mitson

Contents

1 A Not So Silent Night   5

2 Alpine Emergency   29

3 The Battle for Acorn Ridge   55

About the Author   117

Dedication

To Taylor Cox
While we have not met yet, I already love you.
I look forward to swashbuckling adventures together.
"Hoist the colors, boys! And let 'em taste steel!"

Red Team Ink
DBA of Zealot Solutions, Idaho LLC
9480 River Beach Lane
Garden City, ID 83714
Copyright © 2024 by Red Team Ink

All rights reserved. Without limiting the rights under the copyright reserved above, no part of this publication may be reproduced, stored in, or introduced into a retrieval system, or transmitted in any form or by any means (electronic, mechanical, photocopying, recording, or otherwise) without prior written permission.

This is a work of fiction. Names, characters, businesses, places, events, and incidents are either the products of the author's imagination or used in a fictitious manner. Any resemblance to actual persons, living or dead, or actual events is purely coincidental.

For permission requests or information about discounts for special bulk purchases please contact: redteamink@gmail.com. Substantial discounts on bulk orders are available to corporations, professional associations, and small businesses.

Printed in The United States of America
ISBN 979-8-3481-7611-2
Title: The Gingerbread Tales Anthology
Description: First Edition
Editing and cover design by Donna Lane

{ 1 }

A Not So Silent Night

Snowy's eyes fluttered. The air was brisk on her skin, and she blinked in the dim light, first wondering where she was, then thinking about her crew. From her oxidator, she could tell the sun had yet to rise. A bright morning star caught her attention, illuminating the sky to the east. She focused on it, feeling her anxiety fade as the star's brilliance filled her with warmth and reassurance.

"Snowy," a voice said as she looked at the morning star. "There's nothing to fear. In fact, you should rest. I promise you and your crew will be fine."

She blinked again, trying to see her crew in the pale light. Minty and Carter leaned against each other while Goldie slept at Clem's side. Snowy's head felt light as the air ship continued to drift. She wanted to get up, but didn't have the strength."

"Be still," the voice told her as she turned her attention back to the star. "As I said, you need your rest. I will protect you, just as you protected me from the red dragon."

Snowy's eyes grew heavy and she closed them gently, drifting back to sleep.

***

The brisk aroma of peppermint tickled Snowy's nose as Minty poured from the teapot into Snowy's cup.

"More gingerbread, please!" Goldie said, pushing her delicate filigree plate toward Minty.

"One more piece, little one," Minty gently said. "You've had enough tonight. We don't want to ruin our sleep with too many sweets."

"But it's so good!" Goldie whined as Minty went downstairs to the kitchen.

Galileo purred from the corner, kneading his velvet pillow by the window before settling back to sleep in the observatory above Snowy's cottage in Epping.

"Minty makes the best gingerbread," she said. "It's one of my favorite Christmas treats."

"Sugar for your tea?" Minty asked Snowy as she returned with a piece of gingerbread for Goldie.

"No, I prefer honey," Snowy said, drizzling a glob of the thick, amber liquid into her teacup. They had stayed up late to look at the stars and talk about Christmas. But soon the discussion evolved into the usual mish-mash of topics, from ogres and yaks and strawberry tart recipes to bees and flowers and pirates. Snowy and Minty had told Goldie numerous tales of their adventures before they met her at the orphanage, delighting her with each one.

"Remember when we got that?" Minty asked, pointing to a small diamond in the middle of the table.

"Seems like so long ago," Snowy said, inhaling the mint-infused steam from her teacup as she held it aloft. "Queen Luvhoney gave it to us, to thank us for saving her from Pontius Pilate."

The honey diamond began to glow as Snowy said this.

"What does it do?" Goldie asked, her almond-like eyes wide with wonder.

"It allows us to communicate with all the bees in the land," Minty said, finally sitting down with a cup of tea and a piece of gingerbread for herself.

"Wow," Goldie said, her voice sleepy. She pointed to a package, wrapped in brown paper and tied with twine, on the edge of the table. "And what's that?"

"Oh, we nearly forgot," Snowy said, setting down her tea. "That came for us at the Royal Observatory and they had it sent here. It came from Israel."

"Remember that glassmaker who stopped by that day, not long after we rescued Goldie from Heinrich von Brock's telescope factory?"

Goldie shuddered and pulled her shoulders up to her little ears. "Don't remind me of him, please. Just thinking of him will make me have worse dreams than too many sweets."

Snowy rubbed Goldie's back. "He'll never hurt anyone again, little one."

"The glassmaker had that shop under a stone, with the goat hair roof," Minty continued.

"I remember him. What a kind man," Snowy said. Then she turned to Goldie. "Let's open this package and see what's inside. Will you help me?"

Goldie perked up and began untying the twine.

As Snowy, Minty, and Goldie started tearing the paper, the honey diamond's glow intensified. Then it projected an image to the center of the table. Snowy and Minty recognized the glassmaker's voice as he narrated.

"This is my shop," he said, and the girls could see every type of crystal, gem, and glass imaginable. "I want you to see where I work and remember the order of Daniel and the Wise Men priesthood. It's made up of wise men from each tribe of man: Africa, Asia, and the Roman lands."

Minty and Snowy ate their gingerbread while Goldie let out a yawn.

"Soon," the glassmaker said, "you will have necklaces that allow you to see souls, spirits, demons, and angels. They will have thin gold chains and a small cross at the end. When you wear these necklaces, you'll be able to translate strange languages into something you can understand."

With that, the image disappeared, and the honey diamond grew dim. The girls looked at each other, wondering what had just happened.

"Let's open this!" Goldie said, breaking the puzzled silence and ripping open the brown paper.

Inside was a book which looked very old. In fact, it was caked in dust and the binding seemed fragile.

Snowy carefully leafed through it. "This is all handwritten," she observed as she touched the delicate pages. She pushed her glasses up on her nose and squinted at the writing. "And the date ... this is over a thousand years old."

"Who wrote it?" Minty asked, hoisting Goldie onto her lap.

"I can't tell," Snowy said. Then she sat up straight. "OH!"

"What?" Goldie asked, yawning again as she cuddled into Minty.

Snowy smiled and turned to Minty and Goldie. "It says that the author's name is Hiram, and he was a boat builder!"

"A boat builder? I think I like Hiram already," Minty said.

Snowy yawned. "Minty, what's in this tea?"

Minty shrugged. "Oh, it's a very complicated recipe. Peppermint leaves and ... that's it. Same as I've always made. It just steeped longer because I was busy making the gingerbread. Why?"

"Maybe it's the combination of the peppermint and the gingerbread," Snowy said. "I just feel so sleepy."

"What's the book about?" Goldie piped up.

Snowy fixed her eyes on the page, trying to read in the soft light. "Three young girls who travel to ... Bethlehem."

Snowy began to read aloud but within minutes, all three girls fell into a deep sleep.

***

After a long walk through the hills, the girls spied a Roman soldier in the clearing. He was alone, shooting arrows from his bow into a tree. Snowy motioned to Minty and Goldie to wait, but Minty was too excited.

"Hello," she said as she approached him. "Can I see your bow?"

"Where did you come from?" he asked.

Minty smiled and shrugged. "I was asleep and now I'm here," she said. "But I'd really like to try out your bow, if you don't mind."

He looked at the girls, presumably assessing their threat level, then handed his bow to Minty. She fed an arrow into the grip, pulled back on the string, and aimed.

Pffffttt.

The arrow hit the ground a few feet in front of her. Goldie giggled. Minty tried again, with the same result. The soldier gave her a quick tutorial, but still Minty failed.

"Hmph," she groaned.

"Can I try?" Snowy asked.

Minty handed over the bow and tried not to pout.

Snowy's first arrow landed square in the trunk of the tree. She pushed her glasses up on her nose and smiled. Minty rolled her eyes but Goldie clapped.

"Again!" Goldie squealed.

Snowy picked up some of the arrows Minty had shot to the ground and one by one, they all landed in the tree.

"You're a very good shot," the soldier said. "Are you traveling alone?"

"Yes," Snowy said. "We're on our way to Bethlehem."

"Three girls such as yourselves shouldn't be traveling alone," the soldier said. "There are ... *beasts* in these hills. You need protection."

Goldie reached into the pocket of her dress and pulled out some coins. "What if I buy this bow from you? And the arrows?"

The soldier thought for a moment, and then took the coins. "I have another bow and can make more arrows. Be safe on your journey," he said.

***

Meanwhile, elsewhere on the road to Bethlehem, Mary had an odd feeling. She couldn't put it into words, but it felt like they were being watched. A raven circled in the distance, catching Joseph's attention.

"Do you see that bird?" Joseph asked, leading the donkey Mary was riding upon as they made their way to the town.

"Yes," Mary said, uneasy. "There's something creepy about it."

"Definitely," Joseph agreed. "It feels like it's ... watching us?"

A chill descended Mary's spine and she laid a comforting hand on her swollen belly. "Soon," she said. Then she turned to Joseph. "It won't be long now. We need to keep moving."

They traveled on and soon came across a merchant. He greeted them kindly and spoke to Mary, who was clearly tired.

"My good lady, are you not well?" he asked, taking her hand.

"My baby will be here soon," Mary said, pushing her hair from her eyes. "I'm afraid I look a mess, but we are nearing the end of our journey. It has been a long one."

"I have just the thing for you," the merchant said, snapping his fingers. He opened a satchel slung over his chest and pulled out a beautiful blue veil. "Here," he said, "I believe you'll need this and I'd like you to have it."

"Oh," Mary said, touched by the man's gesture but nervous. "This is lovely, but I'm just a humble woman. This veil is suited for someone much more elegant."

"Nonsense, my good lady," the merchant said. "Please, try it on."

Mary did and the veil draped perfectly over her face, as if custom-made just for her. Joseph smiled at his wife's radiant beauty.

The merchant reached into his satchel again. "And sir," he said, pulling out another head covering, "forgive me, but I see the perspiration on your brow. That simply will not do. Please take this."

Joseph placed the cloth over his head. "This is very kind of you," he said, reaching into his tunic. "I'm afraid we don't have much to offer you as payment."

"Glory to God in the highest," the merchant simply said, closing his satchel.

Joseph pulled a few coins from his tunic, but the raven flew over them, swooping down and cawing loudly. Mary shuddered as Joseph shooed the bird away. When it had flown off, they turned around to wave goodbye to the merchant, but he was gone.

Mary felt the baby kick and clutched her stomach. "Was that a mirage? Oh, Joseph," she said, "I'm not feeling well. I wonder if I'm seeing things."

Joseph nodded, wondering the same thing as he picked up the reins of the donkey. Tired, they continued along the rocky road to Bethlehem.

***

Minty, Snowy, and Goldie continued toward Bethlehem. Snowy tucked the bow over her shoulder and stuffed the arrows into her knapsack. Before long, the trio came upon a shepherd tending his flock.

He turned quickly when he saw them, startled at first, then relaxed. "You surprised me," he said. "Are you from around here?"

"No," Snowy said. "We've come from ..." She looked at Minty and Goldie, unsure of what to say. "A far-off place. We're on our way to Bethlehem."

The shepherd took note of their unusual clothing. "I see," he said. "You're on the right path. But I must warn you. There's a prowling lion who roams these hills. I think I injured him last night, but I couldn't find him in the dark."

"We have a bow and arrows," Snowy said confidently.

"But that may not be enough," the shepherd pointed out. "Here, let me show you something." He reached into his garment and produced a sling. Reaching down, he picked up a rock and loaded it into the sling. He pointed to a nearby sycamore tree and closed one eye. Then he pulled back and released the rock, which knocked a twig off a low branch.

Minty smiled. "Can I try that?"

The shepherd gave her his sling but again, Minty didn't succeed. Goldie handed her another rock and Minty failed again. Discouraged, she passed the sling to Goldie.

"Watch this," Goldie said, pulling back. Her rock knocked another twig off the branch, making the tree shake.

"Goldie, you're a natural," Snowy observed.

"I practiced at the orphanage," Goldie said.

Minty furrowed her brow.

"Would you like your own sling?" the shepherd asked Goldie.

"Yes, please!"

"My sister can make one for you," he said. "Wait here, please."

He left and the girls looked around at the sheep and the quiet hillside.

"A lion, huh?" Minty said to no one in particular.

Goldie shivered. "I don't think I like lions."

"Don't worry, little one," Snowy said. She patted the bow over her arm. "We will not let anything happen to you."

Minty pasted on a hollow smile, feeling a little helpless after failing to shoot the arrow or hit anything with the sling.

"Here," the shepherd said as he returned. He crouched down to look Goldie in the eye. "She had one almost finished, so I'd like to give it to you."

"Thank you!" Goldie said, throwing her arms around the shepherd's neck.

"You're welcome," he said. "You've nearly made it to Bethlehem, which is just over the next hill, so it won't be too far. But it's about to get dark. You can best thank me by staying safe."

They parted ways and the girls kept walking. It was getting dark as they came to a hill, and they climbed to the top. As they reached the peak, they stood in awe. A small group of men were camped below, accompanied by fine horses tethered to nearby trees, but they all seemed to be asleep.

Snowy's stomach clenched, and she inhaled sharply, reaching for her bow.

***

The town of Bethlehem lay before them, illuminated by a brilliant star. Silently, Snowy placed an arrow in the grip and held the bow at the ready. Minty and Goldie stood on either side of her, marveling at the star. Around them, the heavens burst with angelic hosts celebrating in song. A sense of wonder and awe filled the air. But Snowy was distracted by a raven that flew over the sleeping camp and toward the town. She turned to observe its path, her stomach knotted in dread, then straightened her back as she heard soft noise coming from behind them.

"What is it? What do you see?" Minty whispered, squinting at the camp below.

"I'm not sure," Snowy said as the raven disappeared into the darkness. Then she turned around, noticing movement from the top of the hill they'd just climbed. "But we're about to have company."

Three men on camels, each leading an Arabian horse, made their way down the hill to greet Snowy, Minty, and Goldie. Snowy kept a hand on her bow, but relaxed as they approached.

One of the men reached into his garment and produced three small boxes, which he presented to the girls. He nodded with a smile and Minty took the boxes from him, eyes wide. He said something they couldn't understand, then waved his hand and nodded again, indicating he wanted them to open the boxes. Snowy lifted the lid and found a delicate gold chain inside with a small cross hanging from the end. She looked at the man on the camel. He nodded once more and patted his neck. Snowy, Minty, and Goldie put on the necklaces.

"My name is Melchior," the man said. He pointed to two of his companions. "That is Gaspar and Balthazar. We're on our way to Bethlehem to bring our precious gifts to the King of Kings."

Goldie held onto the cross at the end of her necklace, squinting at it as the starlight grew brighter, as if pulsing with new life.

"The ... Wise Men?" Minty muttered under her breath.

"How ..." Snowy began, bewildered. "You speak English?"

Melchior smiled. "Now that you wear the Necklaces of True Seeing, you will be able to understand languages that are foreign to you. Would you accompany us to Bethlehem?"

"I want to meet the King!" Goldie cheered.

Minty couldn't believe what she was hearing. "The King of ..."

"We'd love to," Snowy said. "But we've been traveling all day and need to rest for a while. Do you mind if we take a quick nap?"

"Not at all," Balthazar said. "You can use our camp, and when you wake, we'll have three horses ready for you so you can stay off your feet."

"Oh, good," Goldie said. "My legs were getting tired."

Melchior, Gaspar, and Balthazar lifted the girl onto the camels, and they found a spot under a tree, away from the camp of sleeping men. The girls curled up on blankets the Wise Men took from their camels. Goldie snuggled between Minty and Snowy. Almost as soon as Snowy closed her eyes, she was asleep, dreaming about her cottage in Epping. She could swear she smelled peppermint and gingerbread.

"The Messiah is coming," the glassmaker said in her dream.

"The Messiah?" Snowy echoed.

Minty and Goldie leaned forward, watching the glassmaker's projection from the honey diamond as he spoke. "Now that you have the necklaces, as foretold by the prophecy, the sign is manifest in the sky above Bethlehem."

The three girls looked at each other, seeing the necklaces dangling from their necks as they sat at the table in the Epping cottage.

Snowy opened her eyes and sat up. She looked around and saw the three beautiful Arabian horses fitted with saddles and waiting for them, alongside their new friends.

"Shall we go?" Melchior asked.

Minty helped Goldie onto her horse, then she and Snowy mounted up, and the next leg of their journey began. As they rode, Melchior's long white beard rustled in the breeze as he told the girls that he had come from Persia to gift the king the finest gold. "The same gold from which your necklaces were made," he said. Gaspar, a younger man, shared that he was from India and that he was bringing frankincense to the newborn king. Balthazar talked about his journey from Ethiopia and mentioned that he was carrying myrrh for the King of Kings.

Africa, Asia, and Roman lands, Snowy mused as they traveled. *Wise Men, indeed. She wondered to herself if that was a representation of all mankind, from the three sons of Noah after the flood.*

Later, following the star, they trekked through the night. A raven flew overhead and Snowy felt a chill descend her spine. But the star shone brightly in the east, and their traveling party was drawn to it. At last, they came to a humble stable directly beneath the star. It was as if a spotlight in the sky shone directly down. It was something they had never seen before. It was more than a miracle. Melchior guided their entourage toward it, and then the Wise Men dismounted from their camels.

It was just as they had imagined it, just like all the Christmas stories they had ever heard. Snowy could see Mary, Joseph, and a newborn child, tucked into a feeding manger stuffed with straw. Light radiated around them and, as if drawn by an invisible force, the girls moved forward, hearts full, captivated by the sight before them. Quietly, they came down from their horses and stood for a moment in reverent awe. Mary smiled as she saw the strangely dressed girls and the even more strangely dressed Wise Men.

The Wise Men bowed to the king and offered him their gifts. Mary gently smiled. Joseph stood nearby, looking protective and steady. All knew that this was a special time. The girls felt a surge of devotion. One by one, they realized that they were in the presence of something profound, something they may never fully understand. But all was right with their soul.

Mary brushed her veil away from her face and looked at Snowy and the girls. "Would you like to hold him?"

They were incredulous.

"Yes," Snowy finally managed, and each of them took a turn holding the baby.

"This is Jesus," Mary said, stroking the baby's cheek. "He is your king."

***

Joseph adjusted his head covering and thanked them as the girls and the Wise Men left the stable. As they began riding away, a sudden dread chilled the air. They rode on cautiously, all of them sensing something was wrong, but no one could say what it was. As a raven's shrill call echoed around them, they could feel their stomachs drop. Something was wrong. They continued on the path until they came upon a short stone wall with more stones nearby. They turned and saw a field of shepherds, dotted with a few outbuildings and plenty of sheep in various flocks.

Suddenly, there was a blast of blinding light, and a messenger angel appeared. Everyone froze in fear. "Do not be afraid. Or at least do not be afraid of me. I've come to warn you of approaching danger," he said. "King Herod of Judea has unleashed his soldiers, accompanied by demonic forces, with orders to destroy the child. He has ordered that every child under the age of two in Bethlehem shall be slaughtered. He told his men to eliminate anyone who stood in their way.

Goldie shivered in the night and Minty reached over to comfort her.

"Among these forces is the fearsome Red Dragon—Satan himself—who has risen from the underworld," the angel continued. "He is leading an army of men and demons, making their way toward Bethlehem. They could be here imminently."

"We've got to stop them!" Goldie said. "But how?"

"We don't have much time," Minty lamented. "But we must devise a plan."

Melchior's face was creased with both time and trouble.

Snowy's necklace glinted in the warm light surrounding the angel as he disappeared. She looked back toward the stable, then snapped her fingers. "I've got it!" Snowy winked at Minty, and Minty winked at Goldie. Then Snowy looked at the Wise Men. One by one, Melchior, Gaspar, and Balthazar nodded knowingly, and together the six of them pledged to defend the child, no matter the cost.

Two nearby shepherds stepped forward, their eyes wide with terror. They were older than the others, but steadfast and resolved. "We'd like to help," said one. His front teeth were missing and one of his eyes was misaligned. Yet his brows appeared to be joined as one. "My name is Seth. And this is Caleb. We may not have the skill and stamina of some of these younger men, but we'd like to assist."

Snowy sized them up. Where Seth was missing teeth, Caleb seemed to have too many, and his oversized ears poked straight out from his graying temples. "We'd welcome your help, Seth. And Caleb."

She shook Seth's hand, but Caleb blushed and looked away, giggling nervously.

"He's strong as an ox, but he doesn't talk much," Seth explained.

Snowy nodded. "Good to know." She motioned toward one of the buildings the shepherds used for storage. Several carts were parked around its perimeter. "Now, let's go in here and strategize."

The Wise Men, Snowy, Minty, Goldie, Seth, and Caleb huddled by candlelight in the shack and prepared their plan to save the child.

"We have a bow and a sling," Minty said, frowning. "I'm not very good with either of them, but that's what we have."

"Don't worry about that," Snowy said, reassuring her friend. Then she turned quickly, looking at the sky. "I feel like we're being watched. Goldie, do you see that raven flying around? I think that is not a raven at all. Next time you see him, can you sling a rock at it? We need to keep that bird away."

Goldie nodded and Snowy said, "What other resources do we have?"

Gaspar offered his rod and Balthazar a sword. Melchior reminded the girls that their necklaces would aid them in detecting spirits and demons. "You will have an added sense of perception, as long as you wear the golden Necklaces of True seeing," he said. "That will help us in battle."

Goldie poked around in the little shack and found a bolt of linen, sitting on a shelf. "Can we use this?"

Snowy looked at Seth and Caleb. "You bet we can, little one. Great job. Minty, do you have your penknife with you?"

Minty reached into her boot and withdrew her trusty penknife. "I never go anywhere without it," she said.

"Good," Snowy replied. "Because you're about to play a very important role in helping us defeat the Red Dragon. Now, here's what I want you to do …"

***

Minty smiled, confident that although her bow and sling skills weren't as impressive as Snowy's and Goldie's, she'd still be contributing to the cause. But there was no time to gloat. The girls' necklaces began to glow. Off in the distance a heavy demonic drumming could be heard, along with the roar of screaming soldiers and the deep bass and rumble of horsemen approaching.

"The demons are coming, and they're heading this way," Melchior said. "We must hurry."

"Seth," Snowy said, "get some of the shepherds to overturn these carts. That will create makeshift barricades and slow them down."

"Yes, Miss Snowy," Seth said.

"Oh, and," Snowy called after him, "have them herd their sheep into some of these small buildings. As many sheep as they can pack in there. I want those buildings full of wool."

"Why?" Seth asked, confused.

"Sometimes the most effective weapon in your arsenal is the art of distraction, Seth. Trust me. And then wait for my signal." She gave him a wink and a nod to demonstrate.

Seth shook his head and ran to gather the shepherds.

"Caleb," Snowy said, "I've got a special job for you."

He blushed again as she led him up the hill to the stone piles. "Let's see how strong you are," Snowy said. "Can you move all these stones to form a defensive line? You can add other stones if you can find them."

Caleb nodded and flexed his biceps. Then he flashed a goofy grin, his oversized ears wiggling.

"I'll take that as a yes. Terrific," Snowy said. "Let me show you where to line these up."

While they walked down the hill, Snowy pointed out an area past the overturned carts. She explained to Caleb that this would create an extra obstacle. His ears wiggled to indicate that he understood her instructions. As he finished, Minty and Goldie, who had been busy with the fabric, walked toward Snowy.

"What is that putrid stench?" Snowy asked.

Caleb brought his large hands to his cheeks, ears drooping and his broad shoulders sinking.

"No, it's not you," Snowy said. She and the girls turned toward Bethlehem. The moon had disappeared, casting darkness over them. Then an eerie glow began to spread over the horizon, and with it a foul odor they could barely stomach.

"The demonic hordes have arrived," Gaspar proclaimed. "I pray that we are ready."

"I pray that we are strong," Balthazar added.

"I pray that we succeed," Melchior said solemnly.

Snowy felt an odd sense of comfort, as if remembering a voice from a dream, telling her that everything would be fine. Still, she wondered if her plan would work.

The small group stood by, hearts pounding, prepared to fight as the dark forces closed in on Bethlehem. With fire and shadows filling the sky, an agonized shriek grew into a deafening howl as the demons drew near. The drumming and horse hooves sounded so loud now that the earth began to shake.

"Ready!" Snowy said confidently. With a steely gaze, she raised her bow and began releasing arrows. Each one hit its mark, piercing the advancing soldiers. Some fell while others kept charging toward them. A vast cavalry and hundreds upon hundreds of soldiers began to spill into the streets of Bethlehem.

Minty wielded the rod, swinging with fierce determination. With every strike, she slowed the wave of enemies. Meanwhile, Goldie, holding her sling, stood on one of the rocks Caleb had stacked and fired off several shots from afar. Blow after blow landed with accuracy and more soldiers fell from her skilled assault. They were having an effect, but there were just so many of them.

The Wise Men fought valiantly with skills honed through years of knowledge and faith. Swords flashed and horses crashed into the walls of houses while the defenders of Bethlehem, the Wise Men and their servants, stood their ground. The thunder of combat echoed through the streets. But as the battle raged, horsemen charged into the center of town.

"Time to pull the wool over their eyes!" Snowy said. She hopped up on the wall and called back to the shepherds, giving a wink and a nod. "Free the flocks and let's fleece these foes!"

At once, the doors of the buildings opened and hundreds of sheep spilled out, rushing toward Bethlehem. They mowed over soldiers, bleating and jumping with glee as they created a stampede. The charging enemy horses, confused by the onslaught of wooly beasts, halted their advance. It generated enough chaos and confusion for the girls to mount their own horses, each of them picking off riders and delaying soldiers as they raced the short distance into town. The streets were crowded with overturned carts and sheep and horsemen and soldiers.

Minty scrambled up a tree, carefully snuck out over a limb, and jumped onto the roof of one of the buildings. Swinging her rod, she smashed rider after rider, leveling them as they tried to avoid the rampaging sheep.

But more soldiers were coming. And the girls were being overrun.

Just then their necklaces began to glow. All three noticed the raven land atop the roof of the stable where Jesus had been born. "HERE!" the raven hissed. "The baby is HERE!"

Goldie spied the menacing bird, "Back again you creep," she said and launched a stone at him, smacking him in the eye and throwing him to the ground. She could see the demon inside come out of the bird and fly off into the darkness.

"Great shot, Goldie!" Minty and Snowy called out.

Minty jumped down to join Snowy and Goldie. They joined hands and bowed their heads. "Lord," Snowy began, "you know what we are trying to do, and why we are trying to do it. Please send help!"

Instantly, the earth shook. Lightning struck and thunder stopped all movement. Again and again, lightning and thunder stuck all around them. With each successive bolt, a group of fearsome angels appeared, clothed in power, glory, and shimmering light, each more powerful than the last. The angels began to fight the demonic hordes, quickly gaining an advantage. Confident the angels would defeat the demons, the girls focused on the soldiers and the remaining horsemen. The Wise Men rode up on their camels and joined the girls, only to find themselves surrounded by the soldiers.

Goldie gasped in fear as a loud crack filled the air. But this was no storm. It was the Red Dragon himself, his thunderous wings beating as he approached. As he touched down an emerging fireball spreading over the ground, somehow to say that the underworld and the

Dragon were one. His scales glistened a menacing red, his eyes burning with hatred and vengeance. He looked at the girls and hissed, his voice filling the night with a terrible promise.

"I will watch you die, girls" he said chillingly, "and with you, your hopes will die as well. And when you are no more, I will consume the child, devour his light, and snuff out the hope of men forever."

At this, the world went oddly silent.

Minty bravely stepped forward, her voice steady, "Your words are as empty as your heart, beast! You may strike us down, but you'll never claim the victory you seek. For this child's life is beyond you—beyond your power, beyond your reach. You have ALREADY lost!"

"We'll see about that," the Red Dragon snarled.

Enraged, he lunged forward, his tail sweeping the ground with brutal metallic force. Minty was thrown back, a deep gash across her side and blood spilling onto the soil beneath her. Snowy began to rush toward her, but a demon asp rose from the fiery ground and sunk its fangs into her leg. Venom coursed through her veins, making her weaker with each passing moment. As Snowy and Minty stumbled toward a clearing, Goldie valiantly loaded her sling, fighting on, even as a spear pierced her shoulder through flesh and bone, and it stuck out at an odd angle. Somehow, they made their way to the entrance of the manger. With blurred vision yet unyielding determination, the girls—battered, bleeding, surrounded, and gravely wounded—vowed to keep fighting.

"We ..." Snowy said, barely able to expel the words in her throat, "do not ... give up!"

Minty stood tall, wiping blood from her chin. "That's right," she said, pointing straight at the Red Dragon, demanding his attention. "You may laugh now and revel in what you think is triumph, but all the heavens and all the earth will soon rejoice over your failure! Tonight, I say, TONIGHT, in your arrogance, you have fallen short and failed. Not only have you lost, but your loss is so great that even

Hell will shudder at its depth! Other demons will laugh and snicker at you behind your back."

The Red Dragon rolled his eyes, mocking Minty's promise. "Oh, will they? Please," he said, "I'll be the one doing the rejoicing on this night."

Without warning, he swept the three girls up with his tail and brought them to his face so he could take a closer look at them. His nostrils flared as he exhaled and flickered his forked tongue, his breath as hot as an inferno.

Snowy propped herself up, braced against the dragon's constricting tail, while Goldie clutched Minty's leg.

"Ugh," Minty said, waving a hand under her nose, "your breath smells like Hel—"

"Minty!" Snowy exclaimed as Goldie giggled.

The Dragon's concentration was momentarily broken, vexing him further. "Make your jokes. Have some fun before you perish. But keep defying me, and my breath will be ... *Minty* fresh," the Red Dragon hissed.

"Oh, really? Is that what you think, Mr. Trickster? Ha, I bet you don't have the guts," Minty said defiantly, her face in a taunting snarl.

The Red Dragon gnashed his teeth and was preparing to devour her when he noticed Mary and Joseph standing in the manger. Mary held the baby, wrapped in swaddling clothes. She and Joseph looked at their son, the infant seemingly defenseless between them.

"There he is," the Red Dragon growled. "The game is over, and it is YOU who have lost. The Lamb of God, sent to save all mankind, lies defenseless in a manger. And there is nothing you can do to stop me." Then he let out a cruel laugh, his tail shaking and jostling the three girls until they slumped over in his grasp.

Minty clutched her side, still bleeding, and defiantly raised her head. "I wouldn't be so sure about that," she said.

The Red Dragon paused, his eyes narrowing with suspicion. A breeze kicked up and Mary's veil slipped off her wide ears, revealing

Caleb the shepherd, strong and resolute, beneath the borrowed garment. Joseph pulled off his head covering, letting everyone see it was Seth.

"But, the baby ..." the Red Dragon groused. A gasp of an inhale.

Caleb pulled back the swaddling clothes. A newborn lamb, pure and silent as fresh snow, slept in his arms.

"You like that little touch? That's called irony. See, the lamb," Snowy said through halted breaths, "symbolizes the innocence you sought to destroy."

"But you *never* will," Minty added.

"Not today, Satan!" Goldie squealed. The world stood still again as the Red Dragon grasped what had happened.

On realizing he had been deceived, the Red Dragon's fury erupted in a groan of frustration and despair which echoed across the hills. He began to shake, and his grip faltered, causing him to release the girls. As the girls began to run away, the Red Dragon recoiled in anger. All around him, the demons and soldiers, sensing his defeat, began to waver. One by one, they retreated, confidence shattered, the weight of inevitable failure upon them. As dawn began to break, the forces of darkness scattered, fleeing into the shadows.

For now.

Snowy felt herself growing faint, and Goldie rubbed her shoulder which was tender from being pierced by the spear. Minty looked at her side, still spilling blood. She tried to stop the bleeding, but her dress was soaked through. Weary, they clasped hands and fell to the ground together. Between shallow breaths, Snowy asked, "Are we ... are we going to die?"

Goldie's eyes were heavy but peaceful. She smiled faintly. "I seem to remember something ... about those who give up their life ... finding it. I don't think we are going to die, but if we do, there is no better way to do it, than with my best friends and in HIS service."

Their necklaces pulsed with a subtle glow, then dimmed.

The Wise Men, Seth, and Caleb gathered around the girls, making plans to get them medical help. Melchior kneeled beside them. "We have succeeded. They are fleeing. The baby is Safe," he said.

Meanwhile, miles away, to the northeast, at the shore of the Sea of Galilee, a small boat was casting off, far from harm's reach. Once it crossed the water, its occupants would begin their journey south along the Jordan River, eventually to Egypt. Hiram, the humble boat builder who helped them, resolved that one day he would write about this wondrous night, when Mary, Joseph, and their child came to him in their time of need, carrying the promise of salvation to the world. And how three strangely dressed girls, and a troop of Wise Men from far away, bought time with their lives for this small family to escape.

As the morning star twinkled and the first light of day warmed Bethlehem, the hope that Snowy, Minty, and Goldie had defended remained untouched and eternal. Exhausted and finally beginning to heal, the girls closed their eyes, spirits lifted by the knowledge that they had given everything for the hope of all mankind.

{ 2 }

Alpine Emergency

Snowy's weary eyes slowly opened. Still wearing her oxidator, she tried to sit up and look around, but she felt weak as she lay on the deck of the G2. Her leg throbbed and she wondered if what happened in Bethlehem was just a dream or if she'd really been bitten by an asp. The air was cool, but the sun was high in the sky and her golden necklace glinted in the light. Even with her oxidator on, she could smell the crisp scent of a pine forest. Gently, she lifted her head.

Minty and Carter were still asleep, as were Goldie, Clem, and the rest of the crew. Snowy peered over the side of the balloon's gondola, wondering where they were. Still aloft, Snowy noticed a dense pine forest below them, nestled into jagged peaks frosted with wintry white.

The Alps? Snowy wondered.

She had been here before, though not in a balloon. Rather, by yak. Last Christmas, Snowy, Minty, and Goldie made an impromptu trip here to save a village from an army of ogres. Another perilous journey for the sake of greater good.

Snowy's lids grew heavy as the balloon drifted toward the forest and she began to slumber.

***

CHAPTER ONE: The Precarious Bridge

The wind howled as snowflakes danced in the mountain air. They were moving west along the ridgeline of the Bavarian Alps. Snowy, Minty, and Goldie were on foot, with Snowy pulling their yak, Bessy, who was laden with all their supplies. Pots and pans. A picnic basket loaded with cucumber sandwiches, mince pies, and Minty's delicious gingerbread. Snowy's traveling telescope. Some winter clothes for the journey. And various items to help them keep warm and stay safe.

Minty shielded her eyes, peering ahead at the massive rope bridge swaying between two jagged peaks. The jagged rock outcroppings were covered in thick snow drifts. The bridge was long, stretching for a hundred yards, sagging in the middle, and rippling in the wintry breeze. It reached from one mountain top over a massive cliff to the peak at Karwendel. Once they were on the other side of the sheer cliff and could crest the peak, it would be straight downhill to the village at Mittenwald.

"My nose!" Goldie cried, her little face poking through the fur-lined hood of her coat. "I can hardly feel my nose, it's so cold."

"I know, little one," Minty said clapping her gloved hands together to create warmth as the wind picked up and the snowflakes swirled faster. "But we have to keep going. We've got to beat the ogres before they reach the village of Mittenwald. We could see their considerable army and Minty stuck up on them and heard that they would be marching to that little village then up to Garmish. Someone needs to warn the villagers."

Snowy patted at a satchel thrown over Bessy's side. "Goldie, we've written out the warning and are going to carry it to the village so that everyone can read it and defend themselves against the ogres. I want you to know just in case we get separated."

"What are ogres, anyway?" Goldie asked, her cheeks red as if they'd been pinched.

Minty and Snowy exchanged a knowing look, remembering the first band of ogres they'd defeated, along with Captain Savage.

"Mean creatures," Snowy said. "Always angry. Hairy. Smelly."

"*Ugly,*" Minty added. "With terrible breath and sharp claws."

"And, thankfully," Snowy said, "not especially bright."

This made Goldie laugh.

"But," Minty said, "the ogres we're after right now are different from the other ogres we defeated. They're led by an ogre named Blacknose."

"Why is he called that?" Goldie asked, her eyes wide with wonder.

"He has huge black pimples and warts all over his nose," Snowy explained.

"Eww," Goldie squealed, making a sickly face.

Bessy shuddered at the high-pitched noise and let out a grunt. Her shaggy golden hair, dusted with snow, rippled in the breeze as she came to a stop.

"Not now, Bessy," Snowy said, pulling on the lead. "We have to keep going."

While Snowy rubbed Bessy's forelock and coaxed her with a handful of sweet grass, Minty gave more details on the ogres.

"This band of ogres ahead of us," she said, "is a reconnaissance team."

"What does that mean?" Goldie asked.

"It means they're sent to scout the area and bring information back to others, the much larger full army. Also, these ogres have bloodhounds with them. Dogs that track people by their scent."

Goldie nodded, watching her boots make prints in the snow as it continued to fall.

"That's a good girl, Bessy," Snowy said, encouraging the yak as they approached the rope perilous bridge.

"It looks dangerous," Goldie said, sounding a bit frightened.

Minty agreed but didn't want to feed Goldie's fears.

A chorus of barks and grunts came from somewhere behind them. Bessy groaned again and stopped abruptly.

Minty looked toward the forest, knowing the ogres must be in there somewhere. "There must be another group of ogres behind us."

"This is the only way across," Snowy said, her glasses fogging up from her breath. She adjusted them nervously.

Goldie looked back. "We don't have much time. The other group of bloodhound ogres are gaining on us."

"You're right," Minty said. She glanced at Bessy. "Come on, girl. We need you to be brave. You can do it."

Bessy yanked her head to one side, but Snowy gently led her onto the bridge. With tentative steps, they began to cross. Each plank creaked ominously under the yak's weight. The abyss below seemed endless, a swirling mist hiding whatever lay at the bottom. It was way, WAY down.

Halfway across, the wind picked up. The bridge swayed violently. Snowy tightened her grip on the reins. "Hold on!"

Suddenly, guttural howls echoed through the mountains. Bessy froze and the girls turned around to look. Dark silhouettes appeared at the far end of the bridge where they had just been.

Ogres.

"They've caught up!" Goldie exclaimed.

Minty's eyes narrowed. "We need to get Bessy across, now!"

They urged Bessy forward. She resisted the whole way, but they made it. As they reached the other side, Minty quickly looped a rope around her waist, then turned back. "I'll hold them off. Go!"

"Be careful!" Snowy called out as Minty bravely ran toward the middle of the bridge.

CHAPTER TWO: Cutting Ties

With her trusty penknife, Minty began cutting the ropes on the sides of the bridge, backing up as she went. Her hands trembled from the cold, but her focus was steady. "This should give them something to be angry about."

Their footsteps echoed in the Alpine air and Minty could smell their spicy breath as she worked her way back to Snowy and Goldie, sawing through the ropes. One by one, the sections of the bridge began to sag as the ropes were cut. But she could hear the ogres growling in the mist, eager to attack. They were closing in.

"Hurry!" Goldie cried.

But Minty was resolute. After all, she was Captain Minty of the *Gillfish 2*. Even without her tricorn, First Mate Carter, and the rest of her crew, she knew she could handle the situation and stay strong in the face of danger. The faces of this danger, however, were particularly hideous.

"Almost there!" Minty said, standing up quickly. But as she backed up, her foot slipped and she grasped for one of the rope rails only to realize it was the side she had just cut. Thinking quickly, she shifted her weight and reached across her body for the rail on the other side, gripping it for dear life. Heart racing, she steadied herself on one of the last few planks of the bridge. She started to look down, over the ropes, then decided it was better if she didn't.

The ogres were close enough that their mangy hair and foul breath caused Minty's nostrils to curl. But she kept working. Only a few more lengths to go.

Whooping and hollering, the ogres were now only a few feet away from her on the bridge, their grotesque faces contorted with rage. One of them, with a crooked horn and larger than the rest, advanced on her on the bridge.

"Come on, little girl," he sneered. "We're coming for you!"

"That's what you think," Minty smirked as she wrapped the rope around her some more and twisted a length of the bridge rope around her wrist. Goldie, Snowy, and Bessy looked on from the cliff above.

"We will eat you," the ogre threatened, his menacing teeth glinting in the mist as he licked his greasy ogre lips.

"Sorry, this bridge is closed!"

With a final slice, Minty severed the main rope. Sounding like a thunderclap, the bridge snapped and flailed against the cliffside. Minty grabbed even more ropes and held on tight as the bridge swung like a pendulum, crashing into the cliff face on the girls' side. The horned ogre and many others fell to their doom as the bridge collapsed. But several others still stuck on the opposite side of the cliff or near the start of the bridge scrambled to safety.

The remaining ogres roared in frustration as they watched the bridge fall away, and with it, their chance of crossing it.

Goldie clapped her hands, cheering from above. "Great job, Minty! You really left them stranded." Minty climbed up the planks of the bridge like it was a ladder. Finally, she rejoined the other girls and the yak.

Snowy looked down and winked at Minty, who was catching her breath. But there was no time to rest. She surveyed the mountain and remaining cliffside, looking for the best places to set her feet.

"Toss me that rope," Snowy said, leaning over the cliff. "I'll guide you."

The ogres continued to roar on the other side of the chasm, and the memory of their awful scent made Minty's stomach curdle. She started to turn around.

"Don't look back," Snowy advised. "You're not going that way. Come on."

Minty set her jaw and threw the rope into the air. Snowy caught it and told Goldie to hold the end.

"Put your right foot on that little indent, there," Snowy said, pointing to a place on the cliff.

Minty felt the ground give slightly beneath her boot and then began to climb. "Good, now swing your left foot over to this rock."

Step by step, Snowy coached Minty up the side of the cliff. The breeze chilled her to the bone, but Minty continued to climb. Surprisingly Bessy, while bulky and loaded with supplies, seemed to deftly complete the last part of the climb.

When she was a few feet from the peak, the ominous sound of horns filled the air. Not horns like some of the ogres had on their heads. These were instruments used to warn and communicate with others. The bloodhound ogres that were behind them were signaling to the reconnaissance ogres that were ahead of the girls. The echoes bounced off the mountains, growing louder. Minty's arms were beginning to go limp in the cold air, but she couldn't give up now.

"Come on, Minty!" Goldie called from her position near Bessy. "You can do it!"

Determined, Minty reached the top, pleased to see it was fairly flat. Breathlessly, she sprawled on the frozen ground. Snowy and Goldie pulled her up and dusted her off.

"I knew you could do it!" Goldie said.

"Thanks, little one. Your encouragement really helped me." Minty removed her pack.

"Let's have a snack!" Goldie squealed, motioning to the picnic basket on Bessy's back as Minty put her back next to it.

"No time for that, I'm afraid," Snowy said as the horns continued to echo off the peaks.

"We need to keep moving," Minty said. "They're not giving up."

Snowy pushed her glasses up her nose. "Well, neither are we," she said through gritted teeth. Then she grabbed Bessy's reins and patted her hindquarters. "Let's go."

They all looked down and back at the racket the ogres behind them were making on the other side of the divide. They were so loud that at first the girls did not hear it, a deep bass rumble—a vibration. even—on this peak. They watched as the noise the ogres were making on their ridge triggered a massive avalanche which swept down the mountain above them and completely covered them, pushing the remaining group behind them off the cliff or hopelessly trapped in the snow.

"Looks like they got a the white glove treatment from Mother Nature," Minty whispered.

"Yeah they really got buried in their work," Snowy replied.

"Talk about a dramatic exit," Goldie blurted.

CHAPTER THREE: The Ogres Are Coming Back

The girls plodded along the narrow mountain path. On one side, a sheer rock face; on the other, a drop into the foggy depths. They tried to hurry, but Goldie's little legs could barely keep up. As they wound through the frozen trail, the howling wind was interrupted by a new sound: the deep, rumbling bark of dogs from ahead of them.

As they approached a small clearing, Snowy pulled out her telescope. "Wait," she whispered. "Let's see what we're up against."

Through the lens, she saw the Blacknose ogre recon group ahead. It appeared they had heard the horns of the other group and were turning back, which meant they were headed directly toward the girls and Bessy! Snowy quickly made some calculations in her head.

"Blacknose's group is up ahead, and they're coming this way. I'd say they're about thirty minutes out."

"Oh, no! We're trapped between a cliff and another ogre force," Goldie said, her voice quavering.

Minty took a deep breath. "Then we make our stand here."

"But how?" Goldie asked. "How can we take on a band of ogres? We didn't prepare for that!"

The girls huddled together.

"While it's true, we have limitations," Snowy said, "that doesn't mean we're not prepared."

"What do you mean?" Goldie asked.

"Because what we do have is creativity," Snowy said. "Minty, let's do a quick inventory of our supplies."

"Right," Minty said, already making a list in her head. "Let's see, we have several canteens of water, a picnic basket and a blanket, some winter clothes, a little fodder and sweet grass for Bessy."

"Good, that's a good start," Snowy said, checking on Blacknose and his ogres through her telescope to make sure they were still on pace. "What else?"

"Well, there's my penknife, and your telescope, some pots and pans, a small bundle of firewood."

"Good, we're going to need all of that," Snowy said, sliding her telescope back into her pocket. "Anything else?"

"We've got three hand lanterns with whale oil, a flint, a few gold coins ..." Minty looked around and patted her pockets. "OH! And the remnants of the rope bridge."

"Just rope or planks, too?"

"Ropes and planks," Minty said. "As many as Bessy could carry."

"Excellent!" Snowy said. "See, Goldie, we have a lot of weapons in our arsenal."

"Lanterns and pots and pans are weapons?" Goldie asked.

"They are if you know how to use them," Minty said with a wink.

"Exactly," Snowy said. Off in the distance, she saw a clump of snow fall from a tree limb, causing a snow cloud to rise in the air. She thought for a moment until an idea sparked in her eyes. Taking a look around the narrow clearing, she spied a large boulder near the edge of the slope. Snowy met Minty's eyes and smiled. "We can use the environment to our advantage. Come on, let's see if this works."

CHAPTER FOUR: Setting the Trap

Immediately, the girls sprang into action.

"Goldie, take that bundle of firewood and start a fire," Snowy instructed.

"What for?" Goldie asked.

"We'll need boiling water," Snowy explained. "Light a fire and set a pot over it."

Goldie nodded, grabbing a pot and the flint. It took several tries in the stiff wind, but despite the biting cold, she managed to ignite the firewood.

"Good job, Goldie. Now, gather up as much snow as you can and put it in the pot. I need it to melt."

"Can we make some tea?"

"No, little one. No time for tea right now. We need hot water and I need you to keep melting the snow as we go, understand?"

Goldie nodded with a frown but started scooping up piles of soft snow in her hands and dropping them into the water. Bessy backed up a bit, warming her flanks with the heat of the fire. Even yaks can't resist a cozy fire.

"Minty, help me detach the handrail ropes from the bridge," Snowy said.

"Way ahead of you," Minty replied, holding up her penknife as she made another cut across the length of rope. "Are you thinking what I'm thinking?"

"Probably," Snowy said with a laugh, the first bit of levity since they'd seen and heard the ogres, who continued to wail.

"The wall?" Minty asked, nodding toward the side of the cliff. "It's a natural bottleneck, and an area of vulnerability."

"Exactly," Snowy said. "See, you were thinking what I was thinking."

"Yes, and let's save three of these?"

"Absolutely."

Together, they finished removing the ropes and started laying the bridge planks against the icy wall. Then, starting at one end, they carefully poured hot water over the path. Goldie put another pot on the fire and started filling it with snow as fast as she could. Meanwhile, the hot water quickly froze over the planks, forming a slick sheet of ice.

"Perfect," Minty said, hearing the ice stretch and pull.

"Keep boiling that water, Goldie," Snowy said. "We'll need one more pot's worth."

"You got it!" Goldie said.

The bloodhounds' barking was getting closer. "How much time do you think we have?" Minty asked.

"Maybe fifteen minutes," Snowy said.

Minty grimaced and took a deep breath.

"Plenty of time," Snowy said reassuringly. "Let's keep working."

Goldie got another pot of water ready and Minty dumped it on the planks.

"Now the whale oil," Snowy said. They each picked up a lantern and carried it to the planks. Then, following Snowy's lead, they tipped the lanterns and spread the whale oil over the planks and the icy path.

Bessy watched them curiously, munching on the last of her fodder. Meanwhile, Snowy secured a rope around the boulder and tied it to Bessy's harness. Then she went over and told her, "Get down to the bottom of the slope, girl. You can do it. Wait for us there." Without hesitation, the yak plodded down the hill.

"This is going to be one slippery mess," Minty said.

"A twenty-five ogre pile-up," Snowy quipped. "I can't wait."

As they finished, the howls of the ogres grew closer. The ground vibrated under their heavy footsteps.

Goldie looked up, a frightened look on her face. "They're almost here."

Snowy smiled faintly. "Time for the final touch. Goldie, didn't you want to stop for a snack?"

"Yes!" she squealed. "How about some gingerbread?"

Snowy laughed. "Oh, I think we might save that for a little later. Come on, grab that blanket while Minty gets the basket. Then follow me."

Snowy went to the head of the trail and instructed Goldie and Minty to set up their picnic, carefully spreading out the blanket and laying out their food.

"Let's give them dinner *and* a show," Minty said with a wink. Goldie's eyes got wide, and then she had a little cute smile.

CHAPTER FIVE: The Ogre Encounter

Goldie eyed the gingerbread, inhaling its spicy scent and smacking her lips while Snowy passed her a plate. "Mmm!" she squealed in anticipation.

Minty spread a linen napkin over her lap. "Snowy, this looks delightful," she said.

"Thank you," Snowy replied. "The cool Alpine air kept everything so fresh. But I'm sorry we don't have tea."

"We'll have plenty of tea when we get back to Epping," Minty said. "And it will be much warmer, too."

"Almost any place would be warmer than this," Goldie said with a chuckle. "At least we have this lantern." She warmed her hands near the remaining lantern, then bit into a mince pie and rubbed her tummy. "Delicious!"

The girls sat back on the blanket, laughing and chatting as if they were in a meadow on a sunny day. Minty took a dainty bite of a cucumber sandwich, her pinky at full extension. "Oh, this is exquisite," she said. "Just the refreshment I needed."

As she said this, the ogres arrived, their massive forms casting shadows over the girls, bloodhounds lunging from their leashes. Blacknose stood at the front, his namesake warts protruding grotesquely from his knobby nose. His knuckles nearly scraped the ground, and his teeth were crooked and rotten, giving off an unpleasant odor. It was odd, as typically humans would flee in fear, or beg for their lives, but these girls could not seem to be bothered.

"Well, well, what do we have here?" he growled.

Minty looked up innocently and dabbed the corners of her mouth with her napkin. "Oh, hello! Would you care to join us?"

"Yes," Snowy said, "we have mince pies and cucumber sandwiches to share, and—"

"Do I smell gingerbread?" one of the ogres asked. Another ogre shoved him in the shoulder. "What?"

All the ogres exchanged confused glances. "Aren't you afraid?" one of them snarled.

"Afraid? Of what?" Goldie asked, eyes wide with feigned ignorance. "Are *you* afraid? We are little girls, the most cunning and creative beasts on the planet."

One ogre looked alarmingly at another. Blacknose sneered. "Hand over the warning you're carrying to the village, and we *might* let you go."

Minty tilted her head. "Well, that's one option, I suppose. Or perhaps we can make a deal?" She held up the pouch of gold coins and shook it. A jingling sound filled the air, and the ogres perked up. "Stay away from the village and this could be yours."

Blacknose laughed, a harsh, grating sound. All the other ogres looked at each other and began laughing, too. "Foolish girl," Blacknose scoffed. "We'll take the gold and you! Then we'll survey the village's defenses and set up the attack of our army, completely destroying the village."

Minty's expression hardened. "I had a feeling you might say that. In fact, I was *hoping* you would. Just remember, we gave you a chance."

CHAPTER SIX: Down the Ice

Blacknose drew back in confusion, his warts and pimples bobbing in different directions as he shook his head and said, "Huh?"

Goldie smiled. "You should've taken the other offer while you had it. You're about to find yourselves on a slippery slope." Then she started giggling and couldn't stop. The other girls started giggling, too.

The ogres turned and looked at Goldie, wondering what was so funny, and suddenly got very nervous.

Goldie looked at Minty and Minty looked at Snowy, and they all exchanged a wink.

"Now!" Snowy shouted.

In one swift motion, the girls grabbed the planks they'd hidden beneath their picnic blanket and pushed off the edge of the icy path.

"Bye!" Goldie squealed.

Using the planks as sleds, they sped toward the slope, the cold air whipping past their faces as they neared the edge.

"Wheeeee!" Minty said, elated by the rushing sensation. It reminded her of sailing on the *G2*.

"Get those girls!" Blacknose roared.

The ogres charged forward but immediately slipped on the icy surface, dropping their leashes. All the bloodhounds, seeing a chance for freedom, escaped and ran off into the forest. The ogres' heavy, awkward bodies crashed into each other, unable to stop. Grunting and groaning, they shoved into each other. But each time one would get up, he'd slide into another, causing a bigger mess and more chaos. Some of the ogres tumbled over the edge with terrified howls.

Minty glanced back, surprised to see some of the ogres still in pursuit. "They're still not giving up!"

Snowy looked behind her from the crest of the slope. Sure enough, several of the ogres were closing in on them.

"Time for the fireworks," Goldie said, her eyes gleaming. She tossed the lit lantern onto the whale oil-soaked planks.

A wall of flames erupted, creating a blazing barrier between them and the ogres.

As the fire raged, the girls pushed off the edge. It was a bumpy ride, but they reached the bottom of the slope, where Bessy waited nervously. Snowy quickly untied the rope connected to the precarious boulder above. She patted Bessy's flank as the yak quietly snorted.

"Good girl, Bessy," Snowy said. "You did just what we needed you to do."

Minty looked back up the slope, knowing the ogres would reach the edge soon. "Is everything set?" she asked.

Snowy nodded. "All we need now is the right timing."

CHAPTER SEVEN: A Narrow Escape

Blacknose and a few remaining ogres managed to navigate the icy path, shielding their faces from the heat of the flames. Their determination was relentless, just like their breath.

"They're still coming!" Goldie warned.

Snowy steeled herself. "That's fine," she said confidently. "We need to lead them a bit farther into the trap."

"Hey!" Minty shouted, waving her arms. "Are you looking for us?"

"We have gingerbread!" Goldie squealed, then giggled again.

The girls began to retreat along the path, drawing the ogres after them. The ground beneath them started to tremble—a subtle hint of what was to come. But this time, it wasn't from the ogres.

A loud crack echoed through the mountains. The boulder, loosened by the earlier commotion, began to shift.

"Now!" Snowy shouted.

The girls came together and pulled on the rope with all their might. The boulder tipped, wobbling at first, then plunged down the slope. It tore through the path without hesitation, sending a cascade of snow and rocks onto the ogres.

Blacknose looked up just in time to see the avalanche of snow above him, bearing down. His roar of rage was swallowed by the thundering snow.

The girls huddled around Bessy and pressed themselves against the cliffside, holding onto protruding rocks as the avalanche swept past them.

When the rumbling stopped, a thick silence blanketed the mountains. All was calm and bright. Within a few more miles of hiking, they found themselves on a mountainside overlooking the village of Mittenwald. The sun was setting, casting a golden hue over the rooftops.

"We are going to make it!" Goldie cheered. *"Now* can I have some gingerbread? Please?"

But their joy was short-lived. In the distance, they saw the massive ogre army approaching from the southwest valley, their numbers vast.

"Not yet, little one. We need to finish our job and warn them now," Snowy urged.

Goldie called out, "I have an idea." Everyone was exhausted but they heard her out. "Put me and the message on the back of Bessy, and I'll ride her to the village and warn everyone."

"Can you do that little one? I'm sure Bessy is tired."

"You bet! And I have an idea to get Bessy to run down the mountain."

Off in the distance, from the hill that leads up to the mountain, the guards of Mittenwald could hear the weird bellows of a yak, and the clatter of running feet. *And what was that on top of the yak, a rider? And what was that out in front of the yak?*

The guards' eyes bulged as they finally realized what it was as this yak came closer to the city gates. Upon the back of the very excited yak was a little girl, holding a long tree branch out in front of the yak's face. Tied to the tree branch was an entire loaf of ... *gingerbread?*

The gingerbread bounced and bobbed right in front of Bessy's face. Her crazy tongue hung out, trying to get the yummy morsel. Bessy thought that with just a few more steps, the delightful treat would be hers, getting to the village gate in record time. Goldie pulled back on the branch and Bessy finally got a bite of her well-deserved treat as the guards surrounded them suspiciously.

"State your business."

Goldie handed down the warning from the pack on Bessy's side. "An ogre army is approaching! You must prepare the defenses!"

The guards exchanged glances. "Call the captain of the guard here, just in case."

One of the other guards scoffed. "Ogres? Here? That's impossible."

Goldie reached into the satchel again and pulled out Snowy's telescope, handing it to one of the guards. "See for yourself."

The guard's face paled as he observed the approaching horde. "Sound the alarm!"

The fast-acting yak messenger had alerted everyone, encouraged by a sweet and spicy treat. A short while later, Minty and Snowy arrived at the village to help mount the defenses. The villagers had enough time to gather reinforcements from the much larger city to the north, Garmisch. So, by the time the ogre army arrived, the entire valley was like an alert porcupine, ready to strike back.

The ogre army saw this, understanding that their element of surprise was gone, and retreated to the ogre lands. The village of Mittenwald was saved.

Later that day the village hosted a tea party for the hero girls and their yak, Bessy. They cooked an amazing celebratory lunch of gingerbread and pastries and pies of every type. The girls were exhausted but Goldie and Bessy finally got their fill of gingerbread. The girls giggled and laughed together, and Goldie said, "I think I finally understand what you were saying up on the mountain." Motioning to Minty and Snowy, she continued, "Sometimes the limitations help. If you take inventory of what you have, and use it well, perhaps you don't need everything.

"Use what you have well. And use it creatively," Snowy added.

They all smiled, and Snowy took in the Alpine air, warmed by the idea that she would always make it her priority to save others from the forces of evil, no matter how impossible it seemed.

{ 3 }

The Battle for Acorn Ridge

*S*nowy woke, feeling peaceful and content, and looked through the glass of her oxidator. As she removed it, the sweet, fresh scent of spruce trees greeted her. She inhaled and let the refreshing aroma fill her lungs. There were no stinky ogres, no smelly yak hair, no barking bloodhounds. Just serene quiet. A green silk awning shaded her as she blinked, trying to get her bearings. After what felt like a deep sleep, she realized she was aloft, jostling along in the breeze. She bolted up and looked around, her stomach tightening. All the crew members lay still, sprawled about the deck of the G2. Just as her breath clutched in her throat, a loud snore from Clem jolted her. Goldie, eyes closed, nestled closer to him.

They're just sleeping, she told herself. Just sleeping.

Gathering her blue skirt and pushing her glasses up her nose, Snowy took another deep breath and then stood up. Lightheaded and queasy, she was wobbly at first. Her necklace bobbled on her neck. She grabbed the railing of the G2, soaring through the skies as a hybrid airship thanks to the balloon Ari and Silky had mended. As soon as she touched the rail, the memory of Nereus falling over the edge and into the depths of the sea flooded her mind. She thought about Lyr and his handsome, blue-speckled face. She missed him already, although there was no telling how long she'd been asleep. It felt like days, and she wondered if she'd been having dreams, but she couldn't be sure.

***

CHAPTER ONE

She surveyed the landscape below. Alpine peaks gave way to rolling foothills and dark green valleys, amid deep blue lakes and rivers. Farther beyond, densely packed trees clustered together. A large, sprawling castle complex was visible in the distance. It gleamed in the light of what Snowy figured must be mid-morning, given where the sun was situated in the sky. Wherever they were, it sure was picturesque and peaceful. Almost like a storybook, complete with an enchanted forest. And a welcome change from the tense conflict they'd just escaped in the dark, shadowy depths of the Atlantic.

A soft groan pulled Snowy from her thoughts. Minty, who had been slumped against Carter's chest, pulled off her oxidator. Her necklace glinted in the light. She yawned and stretched her arms as she sat up. When she opened her eyes, she smiled at Snowy.

"Good ... morning?" Snowy said, her voice rising. "At least, I think it's morning."

Minty got to her feet and smoothed out her dress. Like Snowy, and any good sailor, she checked the sun's position and nodded. "Well, let's go with that," she said, taking a moment to get her balance before walking to meet Snowy at the rail. "Good morning. Any idea where we are?"

"I can't be sure," Snowy said, "but if I didn't know better, I'd say it feels like Germany. Remember when we came through Belgium and down to Bonn to rescue Goldie from von Brock's telescope factory?"

Minty nodded, still blinking her eyes as she focused on the trees. "Oh, you're right," she said. "It does look a lot like Germany. But we were just in the Caribbean, and that's 4,000 miles ... wait, how long have we been asleep?"

Snowy shrugged. "I don't know that answer, either," she said. "But I think it might've been a few days. It would take at least that long to travel this far, given the air currents."

As crew members began to wake and remove their oxidators, the girls took in the Alpine forest. Then Minty whirled around and looked at Snowy.

"The hole!" she exclaimed. She looked up at the green silk balloon. "It worked!"

Snowy cocked her head, now remembering how Minty had scaled up the side of the ship to pierce the balloon with her penknife, releasing just enough hydrogen to keep them floating so they could ride the air current. "You're right! I bet that's what saved us."

"I remember reading that if you were in deep water for a long time and suddenly came to the surface, you could get something … oh, I can't remember the name, but it's also called the bends."

Snowy clutched her stomach, which was still somewhat unsettled. "I think I can understand why," she said. "It has to do with decompression, and nitrogen in your bloodstream." Her stomach began to curdle. "Uh, actually, let's not discuss it."

Minty nodded, patting her own stomach. "Fine with me."

"Anyway, doing that bought us time for our bodies to regain their strength after being underwater for so long. And the oxidators the Okeanos gave us helped us breathe even with the atmospheric changes."

Carter rustled behind them, sitting up and resting his hands on his knees. He and Minty exchanged a smile, and then he got up and started checking on the rest of the crew, gently shaking them awake.

"You miss Lyr?" Minty asked, laying a hand over Snowy's as they sailed along.

Snowy nodded, remembering the sensation of Lyr's webbed hand over hers. "Yes," she said softly. "But, I suppose it's for the best."

Minty draped her arm around Snowy's shoulder and stood with her silently as they drifted toward the wooded area. As they sailed along, the forest came clearly into view—tall beech, ash, and firs—intercut with an irregular grid of blue water. A very tall, broad white oak tree dominated the center of the grove. Snowy could recognize small streams, rock formations, and a patchwork of clearings as they slightly descended. But she marveled at how it all seemed to lead to the gleaming white oak. So strong and majestic, as if everything emanated from it.

"Everyone's awake and they all seem to be fine," Carter said as he walked up behind them. "How about you girls?"

"Just fine, Carter," Snowy said, turning to him. "You?"

"Glad to have had some rest," he said, rubbing his shoulder. "Nereus was a formidable opponent. I think I took a few lumps. But I'll recover."

Minty smiled at him and then looked back at the landscape.

"Are we back in Germany?" Carter asked.

"That's what we were thinking," Snowy said. "Looks like the Alps, don't you think?"

Minty nodded. "I'd say Bavaria."

"I think that's a good guess," Snowy said.

Just then, the balloon caught an air drift and the ship jolted and started to descend. Goldie gasped but Clem took her hand to calm her. The crew began to murmur as they filed to their stations. Snowy looked up at the green silk cloth keeping them aloft.

"We're going to need to steer this thing down," she said. "Ideally, I'd want to land in the water, but I don't know if that's a possibility."

Minty hurried to her post at the ship's wheel. "Rogers!" she called out. "Hoist the sail and let out the lines!"

"Aye-aye, Captain Minty," he said, quickly executing his orders.

Within moments of being unfurled, the sail acted like a parachute, smoothing the ship's descent as they approached the treetops. A faint chattering rose from the forest floor. The *G2* began tilting again. Snowy looked up at the balloon and back to the ground below, still concerned they might crash.

"We need to open up that hole," she said. "There's still too much hydrogen in the balloon. We need to control the landing but that hole is so high up there."

"I'll do it," Minty said, but Carter stepped in front of her.

"No," he said, pulling his knife from his pocket, "let me do it. I'm taller and can get up there faster."

Snowy nodded while the ship continued to list. "Do it," she said as Carter tucked his gully between his teeth.

With a slight grimace, Carter scrambled up the mast and then swung like an orangutan on a course of jungle vines, working his way to the hole Minty had torn with her penknife. Unfolding his gully, he poised it near the small opening. "Tell me how much," he called down.

"Just a small cut," Snowy said. "Maybe a third the size of the original hole."

Carter pricked the fabric and made a small slice. The ship lurched slightly and then began to stabilize.

"Good?" he yelled.

Snowy glanced over the rail. The ground was getting closer, and there was no waterway in sight. As the chattering grew louder, she looked back at Carter.

"One more just like that and then hurry back down to help steer," she said.

He made the cut as instructed then swung back, dropped into the crow's nest, and shimmied down the mast before grabbing a line with the rest of the crew. Together, they held the ship steady as it drifted downward.

Skimming over the trees now, Minty asked Snowy, "What do you think?"

"Looks like our best target is this farmer's field," Snowy said, pointing to a small clearing in the near distance, shaded by the mighty white oak.

"Steer toward the starboard side!" Minty exclaimed.

The crew, working in unison, skillfully tugged and guided the ship farther downward. The field was in view and the ship was gliding toward it. Mice and rabbits scurried through the field, running away from the approaching ship. The grove was just beyond the field's edge, its stately firs forming what looked like a phalanx, on guard and at the ready.

Snowy looked up at the balloon, afraid it would deflate too quickly, but it was rippling steadily in the breeze. One miscalculation and they could either slam into the ground or crash into the trees. She closed her eyes momentarily, praying for a safe landing.

"Nice and easy," she mumbled. "Nice and easy."

With a hushed thud, the ship rolled across the soft ground, skidding to a stop. Another hundred yards and they would've plowed through the forest. Snowy exhaled and turned her eyes toward the sky, saying a prayer of thanks.

The crew let out a loud, celebratory cheer, only to be drowned out by a cacophonous chatter rising from the forest.

***

Minty felt her chest collapse as she exhaled from her perch at the ship's wheel. A chirping, almost barking, hum met her ears. Filtered under the green silk shade, she saw neat rows of vegetables that seemed to go on forever behind the *G2*'s stern. She hoped they hadn't crushed too many of them in making their unexpected landing. Someone had certainly put in a lot of effort to plant and tend a field this size. Turning the other way, she noticed the edge of a shady forest with hundreds of trees standing like straight-backed soldiers poised for action. Streaks of sunlight intersected the forefront of the grove, piercing the receding darkness behind the trees. But toward its center, a white light emanated, so bright that Minty had to shade her eyes. Amid the racket, it nearly reverberated.

"What in the world is that noise?" she asked Carter, who had come up beside her.

He shook his head. "Coming from the forest. It sounds like … squirrels?"

"That's what I was thinking," Minty said. "But it's so loud. There would have to be thousands of them."

Carter patted the gully he'd tucked into his back pocket, then checked his flintlock before re-holstering it. "Guess we'll find out when we get down there," he said, holding out his hand. "You ready?"

Minty inhaled, unsure of what might await them. But at least, for now, they were back on land. Up from the sea, and out of the air, she liked their chances much better. She nodded and took Carter's hand as she stepped down from her position behind the *G2*'s wheel.

"Start unfurling the portside sail so we can make a bridge to the land!" she commanded from above the din. Within moments, the crew was on the task. The billowing white fabric draped down from the ship, about to create a sturdy overpass. Carter went off to help. As everyone buzzed about, Snowy approached her.

"You really think this is Bavaria?" Snowy asked.

"I'd bet on it," Minty said. "It looks so much like when we first came through Germany, yet I know we've never been here."

"That was such a long journey, making our way to Bonn to rescue Goldie," Snowy recalled. "Seems like so long ago."

Minty watched Goldie keeping pace with Clem as he directed some of the crew members working on the sail. Everyone loved Goldie, but Clem doted on her more than the others did. He never seemed to tire of her endless questions, patiently answering each one as best he could and coming up with new games and stories to keep her entertained. At his age, he was too slow to race with her, but he always played along. She thought about what kind of father or grandfather he would've been had he not devoted his life to the sea. Then she thought about Claudette and her daughters, taking care of their cottages in Epping Forest. She imagined Camille and Annelise running through the meadow and playing hide and seek in the forest, just like she had done at Goldie's age. It seemed like they were so close to home, and yet still so impossibly far away.

"Minty?" Snowy asked, nudging her. "Still with me?"

"Oh," Minty said, her face flushed. "I guess I was just thinking. Sorry."

"So, if this is Bavaria, where do you suppose we are?"

She looked at the rolling foothills behind the *G2*. "I'd say much farther east than France, south of Flanders, nearly to Austria, in fact," Minty said with confidence. She nodded toward the noisy woods ahead of them. "The Bavarian Forest, if that's what that is, sits in the southeastern region of Germany, not too far from the Danube River."

"And the Danube connects to the Rhine," Snowy said with a smile.

"Which would then connect to the North Sea," Minty concluded.

Snowy cocked her head. "So—"

"So, we could be home soon," Minty mused, feeling herself fill with hope.

"Now if we can just find out what that noise is," Snowy said. "And then—"

"Home," Minty said, a picture forming in her mind, one of warmth and contentment.

"Minty!" Carter yelled from the bow, jerking their heads around. "Snowy! Let's get moving!"

They made their way down the sail-bridge with Carter, each of them taking a rifle and a pack of food. Minty sensed the earth beneath her boots and felt like she was in heaven. As much as she loved sailing, it had been so long since her feet had touched the ground, she'd nearly forgotten the sensation. They walked toward the forest, the chattering sound still echoing, although it seemed to have stopped escalating at this point.

Minty looked back at the *G2*. A ship in the middle of a farmer's field was an odd sight. But then, they'd already encountered mermen, kraken, frogmen, and an evil telescope maker who fueled his child-labor factory with pig poop, so she supposed nothing was odd anymore. She stretched her legs to keep up with Carter, who was guiding them. As they walked to the forest's edge, they saw dozens of field mice scurrying here and there as well as an occasional rabbit.

"Seems like a lively place," Minty said. "All these cute little animals."

"I just wish they weren't so loud," Snowy said, covering her ears as they stepped into the forest's shade.

"Agreed," Carter said. "Seems like it's coming from that bright spot over there." He motioned to the left and the girls followed his lead.

Through rows of firs and spruce, she could distinctly see white bark. The closer they came to the sound, the brighter the light became. Whatever was in the middle of this grove, it was large and gleaming.

"Is that an oak tree?" Snowy asked. "I thought I saw one from the deck of the *G2* when we were still in the air."

"Looks like it," Carter said as the noise nearly drowned him out.

Minty noticed clusters of acorns along the ground, crunching under her feet as they trod on. Beautiful blue flowers—nearly the color of the Atlantic—draped over on their stems like tassels. Cottony moss climbed the tree trunks as feathery fern fronds rustled in the breeze.

"This reminds me of Epping Forest," Snowy observed. "Well, kind of."

"Yes, but something's very different," Minty replied.

Just ahead, a thin gray squirrel came sprinting down the moss-dappled path. Breathless and shivering, it stopped behind the thick, knotted trunk of a fir tree, hiding behind a pinecone. It peered back toward where it had come, flicking its scrawny tail repeatedly. Eyes bulging and darting around, it then bolted across the forest floor before disappearing into its depths.

The trio continued toward the noise, which was once again rising. As they did, Minty kept seeing gray squirrels running away from the source of the noise.

"That's weird. Why do you suppose they're running like that?" she wondered aloud. She ran her fingers over the barrel of her rifle and tried to muffle her footsteps.

As they rounded a corner along the tree-shaded path, she ran into Carter's outstretched arm, stopping suddenly.

"Shh," he whispered as she and Snowy paused on the path. "I think I know why they're running. Look."

Carter reached back and took the girls' hands, pulling them up to where he stood. Minty opened her eyes wide, stunned by what she saw.

The gleaming white oak tree, thick and mighty, stood in the clearing. On a boulder just in front of it stood a round, brown squirrel, chirping and barking in an angry tone. Its little fists were balled up, and one slammed onto a smaller rock, which seemed to serve as a podium. Then it reached up and adjusted a monocle over one eye before continuing. With spittle flying from its lips, it ranted and squawked. A small group of brown squirrels stood behind it, erect and solemn. At the base of the boulder, hundreds of brown squirrels were lined up, tufted ears pitched forward, listening with rapt attention as the round squirrel prattled on.

Minty stared in disbelief. Then she realized there were brown squirrels everywhere, perched on tree branches, huddled in groups lining the path, squirming all around them. Some craned their necks to get a glimpse of the one on the boulder. Others merely twitched their tails in response.

The squirrel on the boulder released an escalating string of chatter, punctuating its speech with more impassioned fist slams. Spit flew again from its mouth, the monocle bobbing under its brow. And then, in a piercing crescendo, it delivered a final, screeched syllable. In response, every brown squirrel gathered in the clearing hoisted their fists in the air and shouted a hearty cheer.

CHAPTER TWO

The stocky brown squirrel heaved as he caught his breath, his chest rising and falling as the other squirrels cheered. His chubby cheeks felt warm, perspiration streaming from below his monocle. He looked out at the crowd, hoping to be satisfied with his ability to motivate his followers to carry out his orders. The Great White Oak had been his cherished ideal for so long, and he wasn't about to have it compromised. Tainted by inferior gray squirrels. Those common vermin needed to be eliminated, and he knew he'd have to mobilize his troops to preserve the purity of The Great White Oak.

"Herr Nussler!" a voice called from behind him.

The rotund brown squirrel turned to greet his first lieutenant and police chief, Otto, reaching out for a paw-shake. Nussler dismissed the gesture with a nod. A germaphobe, he didn't like to be touched. No telling what he might be exposing himself to, and he needed to maintain his strength to see his mission through. Besides being highly suspicious of everyone and everything, he also wished to conceal the shaking in his paw which had recently developed. No sense in giving anyone a reason to perceive it as a weakness.

"Otto," he said. "What did you think?"

"Brilliant speech, sir," Otto fawned. He withdrew his paw awkwardly and paused for a moment. "I believe we're making good progress."

"And," Nussler said, wiping a droplet of sweat from his brow, "is your team, the Superior Squirrels, prepared to do what is necessary to ensure ..."

His voice trailed off as he ran a trembling finger through the excess fur over his lips and gazed at the crowd, poised in thought.

"... compliance?"

"Yes, sir," Otto replied. "No measure will be spared in maintaining loyalty to the cause."

Nussler focused on the huge crowd of brown squirrels still celebrating and buzzing with excitement. The adult males stood about four feet high, a bit taller than Nussler. Many were strong, robust, capable of fighting the gray vermin that had begun to overrun their Bavarian domain. They'd come from England, slowly integrating themselves into the Bavarian Forest. At first, their presence was of little concern. But after a particularly harsh winter, with the brown squirrels on the brink of starvation, there was a distinct change of attitude toward the immigrants. Nussler and others had begun to harass the gray squirrels, blaming them for any trouble the brown squirrels had, whether it was true or not. It started with whispers, unkind things mentioned in burrows that soon spread to the forest floor, nests, and tree holes. Little by little, the gray squirrels developed into enemies, even though they wished no ill on the brown squirrels. In fact, an outsider might observe that the gray squirrels held the same values as their brown counterparts. They worked hard to provide for their families and wanted to live in safety. Their English accents set them apart from the native Bavarian brown squirrels. But aside from that and their outward appearance, they were no different.

Soon, however, things turned dark and ugly. Accusations were made.

One night, the Superior Squirrels rounded up a small group of gray squirrels and brought them to the clearing. With no supporting evidence, they were accused of stealing acorns from the Great White Oak. Though the gray squirrels denied the charges, and in fact, every acorn in question could be accounted for by multiple witnesses, they were mercilessly executed in front of everyone.

The message had been received. While the other gray squirrels watched in horror, Nussler and his troops made it clear that any suspicious activity would be met with swift justice.

As Otto rattled off the number of troops who had joined the Superior Squirrels, Otto hid his tremor by clasping his paws together in front of his waist. He had striking blue eyes, unusual for a brown squirrel, but they were two of his best weapons of intimidation. His piercing gaze alone could force any squirrel to confess to something he hadn't done or convince him to carry out Nussler's twisted plans. And he had plenty of those.

The Great White Oak was the mother tree, the greatest producer of acorns in all the forest. Nussler knew that to control this tree was to control the population. And the gray squirrels had become a threat to the brown squirrels' survival. So, naturally, he believed they had to be eliminated.

"And," Otto concluded, "I'm sure you'll be pleasantly surprised by the willingness to join our forces among those brown squirrels who live in the farther corners of the forest. We have explained to them what's at stake, rather intentionally. The Superior Squirrels have been quite persuasive, and the reaction was one of solidarity. I would like to mention that the need to preserve our way of life from these outsiders was a key point of MINE. Furor overcame them."

Nussler glanced at Otto, barely hiding the sneer curling his lips. He knew the game. Otto had always been somewhat of a suck-up, trying to elevate his value for merely doing his job, but never exceeding his responsibilities. He got results, but Nussler had higher expectations for someone leading his not-so-secret police.

"Interesting," Nussler finally said, letting Otto silently congratulate himself with smug self-satisfaction. "And, what would you say is our biggest obstacle in ... *dealing with* these gray parasites who dare to call themselves squirrels?"

Otto cleared his throat. "Well, we outnumber them significantly, assuming we have the cooperation and loyalty of all the brown squirrels."

"And why wouldn't we have that?" Nussler probed. "You said your police were persuasive. Have they failed to guarantee loyalty? If so, we must dispose of them as well."

"No, no," Otto back peddled. "I think it will be fine. They will do as instructed, or they will face the consequences. It was explained in no uncertain terms."

Nussler seethed, annoyed that Otto hadn't answered his question. "Then what, exactly, is the problem?"

Otto bit his lip, then said, "Uh, well, I wouldn't say it's a *problem*, per se. But their leader, WC, is rather intelligent. By all accounts, he is imaginative, dedicated, and brave."

"I see," Nussler said, looking again at the throngs of brown squirrels who were now mingling together as the Superior Squirrels circulated among them. Nussler narrowed his eyes. "Tell me more."

"I suppose his best quality is his ability to connect with the gray squirrels," Otto said. "He is very well liked and respected. He seems to find a way to talk to everyone, in ways they understand."

Nussler felt his paw twitch and gripped it tighter so that Otto wouldn't notice. It was a poorly kept secret, to be honest. Everyone had seen it. But no one dared say a word about it.

"Very well, then," Nussler said. "We will keep a careful watch on this WC and see how things develop. In the meantime," he looked back at the crowd, "we must guarantee that we have one hundred percent cooperation from our brown squirrels. You know what to do if we don't."

A sly grin crept over Otto's face. "I do, sir," he said. "I do."

"Good," Nussler replied. He looked back at the gleaming white oak behind them, remembering the very essence of the cause to which he'd dedicated his life. Such an ideal specimen of fortitude and power. His protruding blue eyes fixed on a single branch, perfect in its proportions, symmetry, and pure, unblemished whiteness. It nearly took his breath to behold such flawlessness. "The enemy within must be eliminated, no matter the cost."

CHAPTER THREE

Snowy blinked in disbelief at the scene before her. Thousands of large brown squirrels, rallying with chatter around their leader. It seemed impossible, but she was seeing it with her own eyes.

"Bizarre," she muttered under her breath as she strained to get a closer look.

"I've never seen anything like it," Minty mused.

"What do you suggest we do?" Carter asked, keeping an eye on the bustling squirrels.

Snowy ran a hand through her blonde locks. "I really don't know," she said. "I'm not sure if I should be scared. Or amused. Or just forget we saw that, get back to the *G2*, and head home to England. But ..."

She swung her head around again to look at the squirrels. Their leader seemed to be in serious conversation with another squirrel on the boulder, looking up at the gleaming white oak behind them. It was as if they were planning something, and Snowy didn't like the feeling it gave her.

"But what?" Minty asked.

"But something's not right," Snowy said. "I can't say what, but I feel like this is too important to ignore."

She felt Minty's eyes roll as she said it, but Snowy was convinced. Something here was very wrong.

"I beg your pardon," came the English-accented voice from the forest floor. Snowy looked down to see a gray squirrel, much stouter than the ones she'd seen running through the forest, tugging at the hem of her dress.

"Hello?" she said, stooping down as Minty and Carter drew back.

"Hello," the portly gray squirrel said, gesturing as if to tip a hat, though he wasn't wearing one. "I must presume you're the humans who arrived here in that floating ship with the big green balloon."

"We are," Snowy said. "I'm Snowy, and this is Minty, and Carter."

"Pleased to make your acquaintances," he said. "My name is WC Squirrel. I represent the gray squirrels of the Bavarian Forest, and we need your help."

Snowy looked up at Minty. "Bavarian Forest," she said. "You were right."

Minty nodded with a smile.

Snowy continued, "Well, WC, what seems to be the problem?"

He looked over his shoulder at the chattering in the clearing. "It's not safe to talk here," he said. "Would you mind walking a little farther, back toward your ship, before we start discussing it?"

"Not at all," Snowy said. "I'm guessing it has something to do with all these brown squirrels and this gathering that's going on."

"That would be correct, Miss Snowy," WC said. "Follow me."

They hurried through the forest, away from the glowing light of the oak tree. As they walked, Snowy noticed small but numerous clusters of gray squirrels popping their heads out from trees and shrubs. Thin-framed and twitching, their beady eyes watched as they passed. Snowy began to feel less at ease with each step, nearly sick to her stomach at the feeling of dread. At last, the group reached a smaller clearing, near the forest's edge.

"I'd say this is a good spot," WC announced. "Do make yourselves comfortable."

Snowy leaned against a spruce tree, feeling its cool shade. Carter brushed some pine needles from a nearby trunk and gestured for Minty to sit next to him. When everyone was settled, WC cleared his throat and began.

"I'm afraid we're facing a formidable enemy," he said. "Not so much this one squirrel, Nussler, who you just observed, but rather, the ideals he represents and promotes."

"Ideals?" Snowy asked, leaning closer.

"Yes," WC said. "Very sinister, dangerous ideals."

"Sinister? How so?" Carter asked.

"My friend," WC replied, "it is the gravest sickness you could imagine. Dark and haunting, deeply disturbing. And all for no justifiable reason."

"Well, that sounds ominous," Snowy said, suddenly feeling a chill in the shade of the spruce.

"I assure you it is," WC said. "And if we don't take action now, it may be too late."

"Oh dear," Minty chimed in. "That sounds very urgent."

"Miss Minty, it is indeed," WC explained. "And that is why I've come to ask for your help. We simply must defeat Nussler and his twisted ideology before he succeeds with his plan."

"What plan is that?" Snowy asked.

"His goal is to—well, there's no other way to say this, I'm afraid—*eliminate* all the gray squirrels in the forest."

Minty cocked her head. "Eliminate? Like drive them out?"

"No, Miss Minty," WC answered. "Much worse. Much, *much* worse."

Snowy, Minty, and Carter sat in silence for a moment as the menacing thought sunk in.

"Oh," Snowy said with a shiver. "How awful."

"Why would he want to do such a thing?" Carter asked.

WC patted his fluffy sides and paced as he spoke. "You see, he subscribes to a misguided notion of nationalism."

"You mean he's patriotic? Proud of his country?" Minty ventured.

"Oh, perhaps, but it goes much deeper than that," WC countered. "Far more extreme, I'm afraid. Yes, he's proud of his country, as we all should be. However, Nussler and those who follow him have taken that pride much farther. It all began a few years ago, when many gray squirrels began making their way here from England."

"That's where we're from," Snowy said. "Epping Forest, to be exact."

"Lovely area," WC said with a smile. "Some of the finest acorns in Europe. Now, as I was saying, the gray squirrels came to Bavaria, fascinated by the beautiful forest and the potential it held for them to provide for their families. At first, they were welcomed. Every year, more gray squirrels came to Bavaria to make their homes. And then, a few winters ago, as often happens, there was a terrible frost. As a result, food was scarce. The Great White Oak, which you saw back there, is the largest, most consistent source of acorns. Even if you couldn't find acorns elsewhere in the forest, there was always a supply from the Great White Oak. But that winter, there just weren't as many acorns as there had been in years past. Now, we know this is nature's pattern. However, for some reason, the brown squirrels started blaming the gray squirrels for the lack of food."

"But that's just how nature works," Carter said. "How could that be the gray squirrels' fault?"

"My dear Mr. Carter, I wholeheartedly agree," WC said. "However, in my opinion, Nussler was just looking for an excuse to start excluding the gray squirrels. Soon, there were curfews set up. All these rules about where the gray squirrels could be, who they could be with, how many of them could be together at a time. One night, the brown squirrels went on a rampage, smashing and destroying the gray squirrels' homes and acorn stores that had been set up for winter. Then there were all these accusations. They said the gray squirrels were dirty, spreading disease. Criminals who couldn't be trusted. When in fact, it was the brown squirrels who disobeyed the law and caused all this damage."

"That sounds stupid," Snowy blurted out before she could stop herself. "Sorry, I mean—"

"No, no," WC said. "You're absolutely right, Miss Snowy. No need to apologize. These were all baseless restrictions that had nothing to do with the law, and everything to do with … oh, again, I struggle to put it nicely—"

"The color of their coat?" Snowy offered.

"Precisely," WC said. "Somewhere along the line, Nussler got the idea that the gray squirrels were inferior because they looked different. It got so bad that some brown squirrels began hunting gray squirrels, almost as a sport."

"That's terrible," Carter said.

"Beyond terrible," WC agreed. "These were families with children who'd played together, who'd lived side by side without incident for many years. And then, thanks to some radical ideas about identity and nationalism, the vicious rumors about unworthiness made the gray squirrels a threat to the brown squirrels. And yet, nothing could be farther from the truth. The gray squirrels want to live in harmony with the brown squirrels. Coat color is irrelevant. In fact, it is our differences that make life so much more interesting."

"So why doesn't Nussler see it that way?" Minty asked.

"I truly think he is afraid," WC said solemnly. "Tyrants often are. I think he feels his own inferiority, as a squirrel in general, and projects that onto others to make him feel better about himself."

Carter raised a brow. "His own inferiority?"

"I don't wish to generalize," WC clarified. "But it's common knowledge that Nussler has some physical ailments that some might perceive as weaknesses in a leader. I don't." He patted his sizeable tummy. "In fact, I'm not exactly in the best physical shape myself. I'm accident prone, and I've had my share of failures, I'll admit. But I'd say that Nussler's greatest weakness is his paranoia."

"About what?" Snowy asked.

"About everything," WC said. "Unfortunately, I think Nussler is the kind of squirrel who, if he fears he can't control something, then he believes it must be destroyed. In fact, we believe he is building some sort of contraption that will help him ... *eliminate* us."

Snowy let his words sink in. She started to speak twice, stopping herself each time to evaluate what she'd heard and try to process such an intent, without success. Instead, all she could do was shake her head.

"It's a lot to digest, I know," WC said. "But that's why, as I'm sure you can see, the situation is so dire. As I told the gray squirrels, I know it will not be easy. But we must achieve victory at all costs, victory in spite of all terror, however long and hard the road may be; for without victory, there is no survival. I promise you, if Nussler is left unchallenged, he will destroy us all."

Snowy had heard enough. "Well, we're not going to let that happen," she said, stepping toward WC. "Tell us how we can help."

***

Minty stood up, then closed her eyes, still hearing Snowy's offer to help the gray squirrels. They were so close to home. Mere miles from getting to the Rhine and connecting to the North Sea. With all the advanced technology of the *G2*, they could be home in a matter of days. Goldie needed to be settled, and soon. But Snowy just couldn't say no to getting involved in yet another cause that wasn't her own.

Tears welled up in her eyes, blurring her view of Snowy, deep in conversation with WC.

"What's wrong?"

Minty jumped, startled by Carter's hand on her forearm as they stood together next to the tree stump. Blinking back her tears, she sighed.

"Sorry," he said, leading her gently by the elbow toward a shady clearing. "I didn't mean to scare you."

"Noah, why does she always do this?" Minty asked, wringing her hands as they stopped about ten yards from Snowy and WC.

"Do what?"

"Volunteer us when it's not our fight," Minty said with an exasperated huff. She paced back and forth, gesturing as she looked at the moss-covered ground instead of Carter's face. "Remember what happened in the Caribbean? We thought we were going to relax somewhere sunny and warm. Then we fell into a giant spider's web and had to fight these creepy frogmen and evil spirits. Then we sailed away, thinking we were on our way home and everything was fine. Then we got pulled down to the bottom of the ocean by seahorse-riding mermen who wanted to recruit us to fight their enemies. Then not only did we have to fight their enemies, and kraken, but their leader, too?"

Carter rubbed his shoulder. "Oh, I remember," he said. "Nereus did some damage, not going to lie."

"And then if that wasn't bad enough," Minty continued, failing to keep her voice from escalating, "we nearly lose our ship and everyone on it, zooming around the bottom of the ocean and then flying out of the water at such a high speed that we need the oxidators to stay alive. Then we fly all the way to Bavaria and crash into a field."

"Minty," Carter said, wrapping his arm around her shoulder. "I know you're upset. We've been on a very long journey, and I'm sure you're exhausted. We all are. Why don't we see if we can get you something to eat from the ship and you can sit for a bit and relax? Maybe check on the crew? Spend some time with Goldie? I bet there's some gingerbread down in the galley."

That thought perked her up like nothing else could. Minty waved and called to Snowy. "We're going to go back to the ship for a little bit."

Snowy nodded. "Sure. I'll be along in a while," she said.

Minty turned to Carter. "Thanks, Noah," she said. "I think you're right. It'll be good to get something in my stomach, and to see Goldie. And I am kind of worried about the crew."

"That's the spirit," he said as they walked back toward the field, crossing through the shady fir and spruce trees.

As they approached the *G2*, Minty was awed by the sudden silence of the forest. With Nussler's giant squirrel rally over, it was now peaceful and quiet. Rather pleasant, in fact. In contrast to the still air and cool shade, the *G2*'s broad white sail gleamed in the sun. Carter hopped up onto the outstretched sail-bridge and then turned back to offer her his hand. She grabbed it and giggled as he hoisted her up. She was pleased with her distinct change in mood, which brightened even more when she saw Goldie running toward them.

"Minty!" the little girl squealed. "Race you to the deck!"

Her boots tromping, Minty did her best to keep up, but Goldie was too fast. They tumbled onto the deck, landing in a heap at the ship's wheel. Then Goldie climbed into Minty's lap and gave her a tight hug. Minty ran her hand through Goldie's dark hair, smoothing it. She thought about the day they'd met at the orphanage, and how she didn't look like any of the other children. But that didn't matter to Minty. She loved Goldie from the start, captivated by the girl's boundless energy. The fact that Goldie was incapable of telling a lie was a mere bonus.

"Are we going home soon?" Goldie asked.

Minty looked up at Carter, who had just walked up, as she continued to hold Goldie close. "I hope so, little one," Minty said.

Goldie nuzzled against Minty's neck. "When are we going?"

Carter frowned and Minty shook her head. "I don't know, Goldie," she said. "But soon, I'm sure."

"I can't wait to have a home," Goldie said.

Minty clutched her even tighter. "I know," she said. "I can't wait either."

Carter crouched down and patted Goldie's back. "We all want to get home," he said. "But sometimes it's not that simple."

"I don't think I've ever had a home," Goldie said. "All I remember are orphanages."

Minty felt her stomach curl into a knot. "We're going to do everything we can to get home as soon as possible," she said. "Don't you worry about that."

"Captain Minty," Clem said, approaching from the stern. "I'm sorry to interrupt, but I'd like you to take a look at something."

Minty set Goldie down on the deck, reluctant to let go of this little girl who had come to mean so much to her. Carter reassured her with his eyes. "I'll look after her," he said, taking Goldie's hand. "Goldie, let's go down to the galley and see what there is to eat, bring something back for Minty. I bet we can find some gingerbread. Sound good?"

"Race you!" Goldie said, running off.

Minty watched as Carter let the girl outrun him, then turned to Clem. "What did you want to show me?"

Clem led her to the stern. "I hope it's not too much of a problem," he said. "But if we're going to get this ship into the water again, I'm afraid we'll need to repair this damage first."

Minty looked over the edge and down the side of the G2. When they'd disembarked into the forest, they'd gone down the ramp and around the bow. This was the first time she'd seen the stern, and there were several long, deep scrapes in the wood, and at least one hole that she could see. It was small, but she'd been sailing long enough to know that a hole of any size was going to be a problem.

"Do you suppose that's from when we landed?" she asked.

"It must be," Clem said. "We came down as softly as we could, but we still slid for a while. I'm sure we hit some rocks in the field."

Minty stared at the damage with disdain. *One more thing to keep them from getting home.* So much for her improved mood.

"Well," she sighed, "let's see how quickly we can get it fixed."

"We'll need some wood," Clem said.

Minty turned and looked at him. "Good thing we're moored right next to a forest full of trees," she said with a giggle.

Clem, realizing what she meant, slapped his palm against his forehead and broke out in laughter. "Well, I suppose that is a good thing," he said.

Minty was still laughing when Goldie ran up to her with a hunk of gingerbread. Carter was close behind with an apple, offering it in his outstretched hand.

"It's not much," he said, "but it'll get something in your stomach."

"Thanks," she said, biting into the apple, then the gingerbread. "Clem says we have some damage that needs to be repaired before we can sail again."

"Great," Carter said, rolling his eyes.

"It's not too bad," Clem said. "I think we can have it fixed by the end of the day if we can chop enough wood."

"There's a huge white oak tree in the middle of the forest," Carter offered.

Minty, her mouth full of gingerbread and remembering the squirrels for the first time since they'd come back to the ship, struggled to get her words out. "Mm, no," she managed. "I don't think we should use that."

"It looks like good, solid wood," Carter said. "Perfect for building."

Minty swallowed hard and wiped her mouth. "I don't want to use that," she said. "There's something very odd about that tree."

Carter shrugged and looked at Clem. "Well, that was my suggestion," he said. "But I'm sure there are other trees that you can use."

Clem and Carter walked back to talk to some of the crew so they could start on the repairs. Goldie hugged Minty's legs and Minty absentmindedly ran her hand through Goldie's hair again. She looked toward the forest, the white light still glowing from the center.

"Very odd, indeed," she muttered.

CHAPTER FOUR

Snowy passed Clem, Rogers, and a few other crew members as she climbed up the ramp to board the *G2*. Each of the men carried an ax, a saw, or some other tool.

"Where are you going?" Snowy asked.

Clem turned back, "We need some wood to fix the ship."

"Why? What's wrong with the ship?"

Clem waved at the others, gesturing for them to go ahead. "Got a hole in the stern. Scratched it up on the landing here. Not a big concern. It'll be fixed soon. We just need some wood."

Snowy nodded, "Ahh, I see. Well, there's plenty of wood out there."

"Oh, I know," Clem said with a twinkle in his eye. "Good thing we're next to this forest, right?"

Snowy stared blankly. "Right," she said. Then she turned around, shook her head at how silly that sounded, and kept going until she was on the *G2*'s deck. Most of the crew was buzzing around, checking supplies, or preparing their posts. Others clustered together, munching on gingerbread and apples. Snowy felt her stomach gurgle. It hadn't occurred to her until just now how hungry she was. She couldn't remember the last time she'd eaten anything.

"Hungry?" asked Carter, offering her a thick hunk of gingerbread.

"Oh, thank you," Snowy said. She took a bite, sending crumbs down the front of her blue dress. She was so hungry she didn't even bother to brush them off. "Everyone's had something to eat?"

"Yes," Carter said, surveying the crew along the deck.

"Good," Snowy said, taking another bite. "Where's Minty?"

"Playing with Goldie," Carter replied. "I think they went down to her cabin. Do you want to see her?"

Snowy chewed the gingerbread, its texture softening in her mouth. "No," she said after giving it some thought. "I suspect she's not too happy with me right now."

Carter leaned his lanky frame along the railing. "Well, you know how she is," he said.

"I do. And I don't blame her. I know she wants to go home," Snowy said. "I understand."

"But ..." Carter said, his voice trailing off.

"But ..." Snowy said, "you're right. Minty and I don't always see things the same way. I think if she understood this situation a little better, then she'd agree that we need to do what we can to help WC and the gray squirrels. That Nussler seems mean and dangerous."

"Look, not that you asked, so please forgive me if I'm talking out of turn," Carter began, "but I think Minty just feels like you're too eager to get us involved in things that, well, don't involve us."

"Maybe you're right," she said, finishing the hunk of gingerbread. "I honestly don't know anymore."

He stood up straight now. "Well, one thing I know is that I'm the first mate of this ship and it's my duty to serve you *and* Captain Minty, no matter where fate takes us," he said.

She looked at him, thinking about how much they'd all grown in the years they'd known each other. All the battles they'd fought together, dangers they'd faced. But maybe they needed to get home. "Well," she finally said, "I'm going down to my cabin."

"Can I bring you anything? Some tea?"

"No, thank you, Carter," she said, then walked away.

In her cabin, she pulled out the little matchbox. Ari and Silky were snuggled up together, asleep. As Snowy stroked their backs, they began to wake.

"Good morning, sleepy heads," she said with a bright smile.

Silky yawned and stretched as Ari opened her eyes and started crawling about. "Good morning," Ari said. "Where are we?"

"In the Bavarian Forest," Snowy replied.

"How soon until we reach Epping?" Silky asked. "I'm eager to see this beautiful place you and Minty have described."

Snowy tried to hide her frown. "That seems to be a very popular opinion," she said. "I think we'll be heading there soon. But we need to make some repairs to the ship first. And besides—"

A loud bang echoed through the air. Even below deck, Snowy could tell it came from the forest, not the *G2*.

"What was that?" Ari asked.

Several more bangs followed.

"I'm not sure," Snowy said, "but I'm going to find out." She carefully tucked them back into the matchbox and secured the box in a dresser drawer. Then she stuffed her spyglass into the pocket of her dress and scurried up the stairs. Minty and Goldie were near the stern, looking over the side. Snowy thought about talking to Minty, but decided it was best to leave her alone for now. While Minty was turned away, Snowy hurried down the sail-bridge and went back into the woods.

She followed the noise until she came to the clearing again. Then she hopped up on the stump and held the spyglass to her eyes. As she peered through the foliage of the thick trees, Snowy could see Nussler and some of the other brown squirrels standing among a pile of white branches. Up the trunk of the white oak, other squirrels passed thick, squatty branches to each other until the last squirrel dropped them down onto the pile.

Well, at least I know what that banging was.

Snowy watched the brown squirrels and craned her neck so she could hear the conversation over the falling branches.

"This will keep those inferior gray squirrels out of our way," one of the other squirrels said to Nussler. "And help us remove them from our forest forever."

"Otto," Nussler said, "I see you're using our resources, but are you using them responsibly?"

"Sir," Otto replied, "the mother tree is an endless supply of wood, as well as acorns. One of the most beautiful things about it is that as soon as we saw off a branch, it begins to grow back. That gives us more ... *ammunition* ... for the cause. As long as the tree stands, we can never run out."

Nussler held up his arm as he and Otto walked along the pile of white wood. The squirrels in the tree immediately stopped dropping the branches while he and Otto examined the pile. Nussler picked up a thick white branch and swung it viciously, causing Otto and the others to lurch back for fear of being struck. Repeatedly, he swung the branch, with the other squirrels ducking out of the way each time. Snowy could hear the branch whistle as it was thrust back and forth. She shuddered to think of the impact it would have.

"And," Nussler said, eyeing the branch from top to bottom as if inspecting a handcrafted sword, "what is the progress of the mechanism with which these branches will be used?"

"Nearly complete," Otto assured. "Just running some tests for speed and steerability."

"Good," Nussler said. "I feel as though we have tried everything to rid our great society of these menacing gray vermin. None of it producing the desired results. This must be the final solution."

***

Minty's necklace glittered as she brushed Goldie's hair. They sat on the bed in her cabin enjoying a moment of quiet. "Stop wiggling, silly," she said, but Goldie couldn't sit still.

"Minty, when we get home, will you still brush my hair?"

"Of course," she said, "if you want me to. But you're going to be big enough to do it yourself pretty soon."

"I don't have my own brush," Goldie said, tracing circles on Minty's quilt.

"You don't? Oh, that won't do," Minty said. "I will give you one. A special one."

"Why is it special?" Goldie asked.

Minty stopped brushing Goldie's hair and thought of being curled up after a bath, her mother brushing her hair like she was doing for Goldie now. "My mother gave it to me," she said. "I keep it on my dresser in Epping. It has a matching comb and hand mirror, too."

"And you're going to give them to me?"

Minty patted Goldie's head. "Yes, little one," she said. "I'd like you to have them."

"Ooh!" Goldie squealed, clapping her hands together. "Thank you!"

A knock on the door interrupted the celebration and Minty got up to answer it. Standing in the hallway was Carter with three cups on a tray.

"Hello ladies," he said. "I thought you might like a little tea."

"Oh, how thoughtful of you," Minty said, gesturing to the table and chairs inside. "Please come in and join us."

As soon as he sat down, Goldie blurted out, "Minty's going to give me her special brush!"

"She is?" Carter said, eyes wide as he raised his teacup. "But then what will she use to make her hair so pretty?"

Minty blushed. "It's an old set," she said. "The one I keep on my dresser in Epping. It was a gift from my mother."

"Oh," Carter said, eyes shifting toward her. "Well, that's very special indeed."

Minty held his gaze for a moment and then sipped her tea. "So," she said, "did Clem and the others get the wood they needed to fix the stern?"

Carter swallowed his tea and set down his cup. "They're in the woods now," he said. "I don't think it'll take long, though. Doesn't look too bad."

"No, I didn't think so, but we can't sail until it's fixed," Minty said.

Goldie stretched her arms over her head and yawned noisily. "I'm so tired!"

"You want to lay down and rest for a while?" Minty asked.

Goldie, elbows on the table, rested her head in her hands. "I'm so tired I don't have the energy to get up."

Carter scooped her up. "Oh no! I can help with that," he said as the little girl giggled. Then he gently laid her on the bed.

Minty pulled up the quilt, tucking it around Goldie's shoulders. "There," she said. "Why don't you get some rest? I'm going to go back to the deck. You sleep and I'll see you later."

Snuggled up against Minty's pillow, Goldie peeped open an eye and waved goodbye. Meanwhile, Carter gathered up the tea tray and opened the cabin door. They stopped in the galley to drop off the tea tray. When they got to the deck, they heard loud banging noises.

"I guess they got that wood and are fixing the stern," Minty said, heading toward the back of the boat. "That was fast."

But when she got to the stern and looked over the side, no one was there. She looked up at Carter, who had followed behind her. "So, what's that noise?"

He turned and looked behind them. "Coming from the forest," he said.

"You think that's Clem and our crew?"

"Maybe," Carter said. "Hey, earlier, you were talking about Snowy. Are you still upset with her for volunteering us to help WC and the gray squirrels?"

Minty shifted her weight, suddenly remembering what had made her retreat to her cabin. It had been nice not thinking about it for a while. "I, hm, I don't know," she said. "I know she means well."

"She does," Carter said. "But I understand your frustration. Seeing Goldie just now, I know you want to get home to Epping where we can ... I mean ... where *you* can give her a home."

Minty searched Carter's face. Wise beyond his years, he had grown into a handsome young man. Strong and brave, yet still humble and courteous. "You're right about that, Noah E. Carter," she said with a smile.

He laughed at the mention of his middle initial.

"You know I'm going to find out what that E stands for, don't you?" she said, playfully poking a finger into his chest.

"We'll see," he said, gently brushing her hand away and holding it briefly.

"Carter!" a shout came from the starboard side.

He dropped Minty's hand and whirled around.

Two crew members motioned for him to join them. "We need help coiling up this rigging! It must've gotten tangled while we were in the air!"

"Be right there!" Carter replied. He turned back to Minty. "Seriously, I just want you to know I understand why you're so reluctant to help. Now, I'm going to go help over there. Why don't you take it easy, or at the very least, stay out of trouble?"

Minty smiled. "Why start now?"

More banging came from the woods as they laughed. Minty's eyes shifted to the dark forest. She wondered what could make such a noise.

"Stay out of trouble," he said. "I mean it."

She batted her eyelashes and smirked. He shook his head and went to help with the rigging. Minty watched him momentarily, then slipped along the portside of the ship, chatting with various crew members. Then, looking back to see that Carter had his back to her, she snuck down the sail-bridge and hurried toward the forest. The banging got louder, and it seemed to be coming from the direction of the white oak tree where they'd seen Nussler delivering his speech.

"Hey!"

Minty stopped in a clearing, startled by the loud whisper.

"Over here!" Snowy called. "You have to see this!"

Minty stepped carefully, silencing her footsteps, to join Snowy between two trees. Silently, she accepted the spyglass Snowy was offering her and looked through the eyepiece. There were Nussler, Otto, and other brown squirrels, chatting around a pile of wood, with branches being dropped at a steady rate. The source of the loud banging.

"What are they doing?" Minty asked.

"You won't believe this," Snowy said. "From what I've heard, it sounds like they're building some sort of machine to wipe out the gray squirrels."

"Machine? What's the wood for? Do they burn it to power the machine?"

Snowy swallowed hard. "No. Something much worse."

Minty wrinkled her brows. "Worse?"

Snowy pointed to Nussler and the others. When Minty looked over, he took a thick branch and swung it forcefully. It met the spine of a brown squirrel with such vicious intensity that a loud crack echoed throughout the forest. The squirrel went down, yelping in pain, its brown body spasming uncontrollably. Nussler and Otto chuckled and nodded.

"Oh yes," Nussler said, placing his foot on the shoulder of the still-twitching squirrel. His bulging blue eyes lit up as if he'd just unwrapped his favorite toy at Christmas. "This will do nicely."

Minty felt her stomach tighten. "Oh dear," she gasped.

"That's what the wood from the Great White Oak is for," Snowy confirmed. "To beat the gray squirrels until they've all been eliminated."

Fighting back a wave of nausea, Minty said, "Then that settles it."

Snowy raised a brow. "Oh?"

Minty stood tall. "We're going to stay and fight."

CHAPTER FIVE

Nussler shoved his foot farther into the twitching squirrel's shoulder, oblivious to his yelps of pain. Eyes fixed on the gleaming white branch, he admired its heft and the velocity it created. These branches were going to change their strategy against the gray squirrels, without a doubt.

"Sir," Otto said, "I trust you're pleased?"

"Very much," Nussler said. The injured squirrel gasped for breath and Nussler removed his foot, then stepped over him, with Otto following behind. "How quickly can we get these fitted onto the machine and put it to use?"

"That's hard to say," Otto replied.

Nussler's round, protruding eyes pierced Otto with their steely blue gaze. He'd had more than enough of this lack of commitment. "Give me an answer," he spat in a clipped tone.

Otto shook. "I ... I'd think they'd be able to start that work later today. We need to transport the branches to the machine. I don't think it's wise to bring the machine here. At least not yet. And then of course, we have the matter of crossing the stream to get to the machine. So that will take some time—"

"Which we *don't have*," Nussler snapped. He felt his tremor accelerate and quickly clasped his other paw over the one afflicted. "Get this underway immediately. And in the meantime, since you can't seem to be trusted to figure these things out, I've come up with a plan to lure WC, and all his little lemmings, out into the open so that we'll have the most favorable conditions."

"Oh, do tell, sir!" Otto shifted his weight, grateful to have pivoted away from Nussler's grilling. For now.

Nussler closed his eyes and inhaled deeply. The Bavarian Forest was such a pure and special place. The air was clean and crisp, unsullied by pollution. The trees, the streams, the wildlife—all a testament to generations of survival and success. A perfect setting for their perfect community, where brown squirrels could thrive and enjoy all the best that life had to offer. And soon, it would be rid of these bothersome vermin that had invaded their blissful nirvana. Basking in the glow of the Great White Oak, he pictured the glorious reward that awaited him.

"Otto," Nussler began, "for too long, we have allowed these gray squirrels to live among us. We greeted them as friends, sharing our food and shelter here in the forest. We'd had few problems before they arrived. And then, not so coincidentally, food was scarce. Disease spread. Our brown squirrels began to suffer in ways they'd never suffered before. These gray squirrels are a scourge on our great society. We have tried to reason with them, but the time for reasoning is over. To preserve our master species, we must eliminate these pests once and for all."

Otto blinked. "Yes, sir, I agree," he said. "But pray tell, what is your plan?"

Nussler shot him a glance. He didn't appreciate being rushed when he was building important momentum in conversation. All throughout Bavaria, he was known for his powerful storytelling, even though he had been banned from making speeches here. Nevertheless, his way with words had motivated thousands of squirrels to act in support of his ideas. He wasn't about to let his second-in-command deprive him of his glory now.

"My *plan*," Nussler said, leaning close to Otto's furry brown face, "is to invite WC to sign a peace treaty."

"A peace treaty, sir? But then why do we need the mach—*ahh, I see*," Otto said as the thought settled into his mind.

"Out in the open, at the edge of the forest," Nussler said. "We'll tell WC to bring all the gray squirrels to this historic event, so that they all may witness history. I'll make up some story about wanting to share the forest with them. They're dumb enough to believe that." His voice began to escalate with great fury. "And with them all gathered to watch the peace treaty being signed, our machine will descend upon them and attack. No gray squirrel will be spared, not even the sows or kits. Our machine will slaughter every one of them, taking no prisoners!"

Spittle flew from his lips and his pulse raced. Wiping the sweat from his brow, he felt his chest heave with excitement over his brilliant plan. His tremor accelerated again, but he was unconcerned at this point. This plan would surely eliminate the gray squirrel problem, leaving the brown squirrels to rule the forest again. And he would be their savior, the squirrel who made this blessing possible. All throughout Bavaria, squirrels would fall on their knees to greet him and thank him for this noble act. Absentmindedly, Nussler rubbed his paws together, visualizing his dream coming true.

"It's a brilliant plan," Otto said fawningly. "We'll get right to work on transporting these branches down to the machine. Again, I believe the stream is the biggest obstacle, but it shouldn't take more than a day or two. When is this supposed peace treaty signing to take place?"

Nussler spun and looked at Otto. Finally, some cooperation. Refreshing. "I'll send a messenger to him in short order. Shall we say, this evening, just before sunset? That should give you sufficient time to load all the branches on the machine."

"This evening? Sir, I—"

"Make it happen, Otto," Nussler said, turning on his heel and reversing course. He nearly tripped over the injured squirrel who was still sprawled on the ground. As he regained his balance, he kicked the squirrel in the shoulder, eliciting a loud groan. "This evening. Be ready."

Otto saluted as Nussler stomped away toward a small group of Superior Squirrels, officers in Nussler's army.

"Fritz!" Nussler yelled. "I need you to deliver a message!"

CHAPTER SIX

Snowy sat in the afternoon sun on the deck of the *G2*. Sipping a cup of tea, she leafed through her notebook, reviewing the messages she'd scribbled to herself and the calculations she'd made during their underwater adventure. It seemed like so long ago that she'd spent time with Lyr, and she missed his silly wit and strong leadership. But, she knew he'd want her to use her intellect to help WC and the gray squirrels in their conflict with Nussler and his brown squirrels. The stern had been repaired. They'd be ready to go as soon as this little diversion was over. But first, she had to come up with a plan.

Finding a blank page, she sketched the forest as well as she could remember it, putting a stream at one end, the field where the *G2* had landed at the other, and the Great White Oak in the center. Her stomach turned again as she thought about the way Nussler intended to use its branches. It seemed a shame to use such a beautiful living thing for a purpose so evil and wicked.

"What are you working on?" Minty asked, walking up beside her.

"Oh," Snowy said, startled, "just thinking about how to help the gray squirrels. I think we'll need to provide some sort of cover for them, but I'm not sure how yet. Trying to get some ideas."

"I see," Minty said. "I don't know if you heard, but Clem and the others have fixed the damage to the stern."

"I did hear," Snowy said, pushing her glasses up her nose. "That's great. We can get home soon."

Minty looked toward the forest. "Well, whenever we're done here."

Snowy smiled. "I know you don't want to be here," she said. "I understand. But you know it's the right thing to do."

"No, you're right," Minty said. "I *do* want to get home. That's no secret. But I saw it for myself. Nussler is a tyrant with sick ideas. We have to help WC."

"Miss Snowy!" called a voice from the edge of the forest.

She looked past the bow to see WC standing on a rock and waving his arms and holding something.

"Miss Snowy!" he repeated. "I have urgent news!"

Snowy grabbed her notebook and ran to the bow. "What is it? What's that you're holding?"

"It's the most startling development," WC called. "Nussler wants to sign a peace treaty."

Snowy blinked. "A ... *peace treaty?* Really?"

"Oh yes," WC said, holding up a piece of paper. "It says so right here in his message. He had it delivered a short time ago. I can't believe this turn of events. He's willing to set our differences aside and allow the gray squirrels to live side by side with the brown squirrels. He has asked that I gather up all the gray squirrels and bring them with me. All we have to do is meet in the clearing near the big white oak tree, this evening and sign the treaty."

Snowy's stomach churned. This seemed rather suspicious given what she and Minty had just seen in the forest earlier that day.

"Isn't it wonderful news?" WC called.

"Uh," Snowy said, unable to put any words together. "I, uh, I think it's—"

Suddenly aware that Nussler or his Superior Squirrels spies might be listening, she stopped herself from sharing her thoughts out loud.

"You know what? I'm going to come down there and then we can discuss it," she said. "Give me a few minutes."

"Of course," WC said. "But don't take too long. I want to be sure we have everyone there on time."

Snowy nodded and turned to Minty. "Are you thinking what I'm thinking?"

"That it's a trap?" Minty asked. "Yes."

Snowy ran her hands through her hair, her thoughts coming rapidly as she tried to figure out what they'd need. Going through a list in her head, she hurried across the deck. "Gather up Carter, Clem, Rogers, and a few others," she instructed. "Meet me at the clearing."

"That's it? That's the plan?"

"We don't really have any time to plan," Snowy said, quickly loading her rifle. "Get your weapons and anything else you can carry that might be helpful and meet us in the clearing. We'll just have to wing it."

With that, she hurried down the sail-bridge. As she stepped onto the grass, she saw Clem, who was having a picnic with Goldie in front of the ship. He raised a teacup as she passed.

"Everything alright?" he asked, a crown of white and yellow daisies slipping off his temple. Goldie, with gloves on her hands, fiddled with more flowers and tried to link their stems together.

"Oh, Clem," Snowy said, surprised. "I thought you were still on the ship. Go see Minty and get ready to meet me in the clearing."

"The clearing?"

"Minty will know," she said, her pace quickening. "Just ... we'll need all the help we can get."

Clem nodded as Goldie gathered the teacups. She packed them into a little satchel she'd brought. Snowy recognized it as Goldie's place for storing various treasures, like marbles, buttons, and other odd things she found wherever she went.

Snowy continued toward the forest's edge until she met WC, who was still on the rock.

"Miss Snowy," he said, "why do you have your rifle?"

"Can't be too careful," she said. "Can I see the message you received from Nussler?"

"Of course," he said, handing it to her.

She scanned the text, which was filled with flowery language about setting differences aside and living in harmony. Words she couldn't imagine Nussler ever thinking, let alone putting down on paper.

"Isn't it wonderful?" WC asked. "A lovely ceremony to celebrate peace."

Snowy glanced at him. "Actually," she said, "I have my doubts. I think this is a trick, and I think your squirrels need to be ready to fight."

"Fight?" WC drew back at the word. "Oh, I do hope it doesn't come to that."

"We're going to need more than hope," Snowy said, handing the message back to him. "You think the brown squirrels outnumber the gray squirrels?"

"I'd say it's about even. But, I can't be sure."

Snowy thought for a minute. "Here's what we're going to do," she said. "Get all the gray squirrels. ALL of them. Then head to the clearing. BUT ... only bring about a third of them forward. Have the rest hide in the trees."

"Very well," WC said. "I'll round them up and then meet you there."

As Snowy got to the edge of the forest, she saw Minty, Carter, and a few others descending the sail-bridge. Since they were so close, she decided to wait. Clem and Goldie brought up the rear.

"Goldie," Snowy said when the group reached her, "I'm not sure you should be here. It could be dangerous."

"I want to help!" she cried, her satchel slung over one shoulder.

"I'll keep an eye on her," Clem said.

Snowy frowned. There wasn't time to send Goldie back to the ship, and she didn't want her going back by herself anyway. "Alright," she said reluctantly. "Let's get going. The ceremony should be starting soon."

They made their way toward the clearing, being as quiet as possible. Everywhere Snowy looked, gray squirrels were tucking themselves behind rocks or into hollowed out tree trunks. The *G2* crew took their positions in the spot where Snowy and Minty had hidden earlier. With her spyglass, she watched as Nussler, Otto, and WC took their places in front of the Great White Oak. Hundreds of gray squirrels gathered around the edge of the clearing, chattering away.

Meanwhile, with several rows of brown squirrels silently lined up behind Nussler, he stepped forward.

"My friends," he said, as the chattering died down.

Each of the brown squirrels raised an arm, "Herr Nussler!" they said in unison.

Nussler gestured for them to put their arms down. "My friends," he repeated, "we are here for a special occasion. As you know, the gray squirrels, who have emigrated from England, are joining us today. Their leader, WC Squirrel, is here to do something that has been a long time coming."

WC smiled, shifting his weight. Snowy thought he looked uneasy. But a soft rumbling drew her attention elsewhere.

"What's that noise?" Minty whispered.

Nussler gestured to the brown squirrels behind him, who immediately began to applaud. The noise drowned out the rumbling.

Snowy peered through the spyglass, scanning the forest. Coming up from the stream was a vehicle, slowly rolling over the uneven ground. Two thick brown squirrels rode on the top. Attached to each side was a shelf, stacked with white branches.

Gasping, she turned the spyglass back to WC whose ears had begun to twitch. Surely, he must have detected the noise. He stood close to Nussler now, shaking paws as the gray squirrels joined in the applause and began to chatter.

"Of course," Snowy said. "Nussler knew that would keep them from hearing his machine."

"What machine?" Minty whispered. "What's happening?"

Snowy turned back and saw the machine roll to a stop, hidden behind the Great White Oak where another group of brown squirrels formed a phalanx.

"They're going to attack the gray squirrels with a machine," Snowy said.

But before anyone could react, Nussler held up his paw and silenced the crowd. The brown squirrels behind him tightened their stance, closing any gaps between them. More rows of brown squirrels emerged from the forest, encircling the gray squirrels. "WC Squirrel," he said, "we have a surprise for you."

Snowy heard the machine start again and it began rumbling toward the clearing. Each of the squirrels on the top began feeding branches into the machine's side ports, wielding them like clubs as it rolled toward the gray squirrels.

Nussler continued, "I have asked you here for this historic event. And now, it is my pleasure, to request—no, to *demand*—your unconditional surrender."

"NUTS!" WC yelled. "Retreat and take your positions!"

***

Minty watched in horror as the machine rumbled up from behind the Great White Oak and started swinging branches at the gray squirrels. Sickening thwacks resounded through the forest, followed by shrieks and frenzied chatter. As the unsuspecting gray squirrels began to fall, swarms of brown squirrels emerged from the deeper recesses of the woods and began punching, kicking, and scratching the squirrels the machine couldn't yet reach. They were piling up in heaps, much to the delight of Nussler and his troops, who stood and laughed at the carnage.

"Oh no!" Minty screamed. "We have to stop this!"

More noise behind her caused her to spin around. As the machine plowed through the gray squirrels in front of them, scores of brown squirrels had come down from the streambed and begun to attack the gray squirrels who had been hiding. It was an assault on all fronts, with no escape in sight.

WC Squirrel called out, "You *quisling!*"

"Quisling?" asked Nussler. "What does that mean?"

"TRAITOR!" WC replied. "You gave your word that there would be peace at last and then you betrayed us!"

"And you were foolish enough to believe it," Nussler snapped, pushing his round face into WC's. The monocle balanced on his fleshy cheek bobbed as he spoke his hateful words. "That is a true testament to your species' inferior intellect. My plan worked perfectly, and you fell into my trap without hesitation, thanks to your naïve incompetence. It will give me great pleasure to watch as you witness your population's complete decimation. And when we win the Battle of Acorn Ridge, the brown squirrels will rule the Bavarian Forest once again, just as it was always intended to be."

"Buzz off! We shall not flag or fail," WC announced. "We shall go on to the end. We shall never surrender."

He balled up his fists and stepped toward Nussler, but Otto and other members of the Superior Squirrels restrained him. As he struggled to break free, Otto punched him in his furry jaw. WC reeled back, barely staying upright. One of the Superior Squirrels landed a second brutal punch to WC's jaw. As he slid to the ground, the Superior Squirrels released their grip, depositing him at the base of the Great White Oak in a heap. Minty saw him twitch and then his eyes rolled back in his head as he gasped for breath.

By now, total mayhem had broken out in the clearing and beyond. The machine continued to shove its way through the screeching gray squirrels, smacking them into submission as the brown squirrels on top fed more branches into the machine's sides. Minty was appalled by the vicious devastation all around her.

But Goldie's screams snapped her back to reality.

"There are so many of them!" cried the little girl. "We're surrounded!"

Minty looked around. It was true. Everywhere she looked, the squirrels were locked in combat.

Snowy grabbed her rifle and began to aim it at Nussler. As she did, WC tried getting to his feet, stumbling toward the chubby brown squirrel.

"Wait!" Minty yelled, throwing up her arms. "You don't have a clean shot! You might hit WC!"

Snowy lowered the rifle. "We need to do something! They're slaughtering the gray squirrels!"

As she said it, the ground began to shake. Nussler's savage machine was heading this way, mercilessly rolling over everything in its path.

"We have to fall back for now," Minty urged, grabbing Goldie's hand. "Let's get a plan in place before we do something foolish."

They ran through the woods, dropping down and circling back toward the Great White Oak. The sound of the burbling stream grew louder as the rumbling began to fade. Minty spied a thick tree stump, surrounded by fallen, moss-covered branches, and ran toward it, pulling Goldie along. As they approached the stump, Minty caught her foot in a gopher hole. She stumbled forward, straight into Carter's arms.

"Don't worry," he said, holding her up. "I'm not going to let that hole swallow you up."

Minty looked at the ground. "That's it!"

Snowy cocked her head. "What?"

"Carter," Minty asked, stepping out of his arms and looking at the path above them that lead toward the stream. "How fast can you dig two holes? One in front of these branches and one behind the stump."

The machine lurched closer.

"I'll help," Clem said.

They each grabbed a rifle, using the butt end to dig into the ground.

"Oh," Snowy said, eyeing the path. She turned back to Minty, and they exchanged a wink. "I see what you're doing. Good thinking, my friend."

Minty heard the machine changing direction, heading straight for them. As the hole behind the stump grew bigger, Snowy motioned for the hiding gray squirrels to jump in and take cover.

"Help us dig!" Minty instructed the squirrels. Then she jumped onto the stump and waved her arms.

As the gray squirrels filed into the hole behind the stump, each one helped to dig deeper and wider. The machine kept rumbling, creeping closer and striking at any gray squirrel within its reach.

Minty tried to get a better look at it from her perch atop the stump. As the machine wound its way through the trees, Minty heard Nussler laughing. When it emerged from behind the spruce trees, she could see that he was riding on top of the machine, with WC laying at his feet, and her stomach soured.

"I can't go any faster," Clem fretted, still jamming his rifle into the dirt, and digging with his bare hands. "This hole won't be deep enough to hold the machine."

"Doesn't have to be," Snowy said. "Just needs to be wide enough and deep enough to slow it down."

Carter hopped over the stump and started digging next to Clem, soft earth flying into the air as they made a trench.

"Dig toward the stream," Snowy instructed and the other crew members got to work. "Connect this trench to the path."

"Goldie, I need your help," Minty said. "Do you think you can do some cartwheels with me?"

"You bet I can!" she squealed.

"Can you do cartwheels uphill?"

"Ooh!" she squealed again. "I've never done that before. Let's try it!"

Goldie clapped her hands together with such excitement that her satchel slipped off her shoulder, falling open near Snowy's feet. Snowy looked inside the satchel. Then she looked at the stream a short distance away and smiled.

"Nussler thought he'd get away with this, but it's going to be a slippery slope," Snowy said, remembering their last Alpine adventure with Bessy and the ogres.

"What does that mean?" Carter asked, dirt and moss stuck in his hair.

Minty laughed. "You'll see." Then she turned to Goldie. "Are you ready?"

"Ready!"

"You can't catch us!" Minty called to Nussler. "Come and get us!"

Goldie giggled as she echoed Minty's words, her necklace gleaming. "Come and get us!"

With the last of the gray squirrels funneling into the ditch behind the stump, Minty and Goldie began cartwheeling along the path that led toward the stream.

CHAPTER SEVEN

Nussler's protruding eyes widened, fixed on the tumbling girls on the path. Though surprised to see them, he realized it would be just like these inferior gray squirrels to rely on assistance from humans. Here he was on the brink of eliminating these vermin and claiming the brown squirrels' rightful place at the elite level of society. He had not worked this hard to be deterred by human interference. All his life, he had encountered setbacks and felt inadequate. So many failings, so many shortcomings, so much ridicule from those who didn't understand his true capabilities and intentions. In school, he had been teased mercilessly. Bullied to the point of maddening frustration, inspiring a desire for revenge and shaping his vision of supremacy. But now he was finally getting the recognition he deserved and employing his plan to establish the dominance of the brown squirrels for generations to come. He wasn't about to let these humans ruin his chances. They must be eliminated as well.

"Follow them!" he ordered as the machine loped through the rows of trees. "Do not let them out of your sight!"

He was so focused, he didn't hear WC Squirrel groan below his foot, slowly regaining consciousness. The machine rumbled toward a thick, fallen branch.

"You can't catch us!" the two girls repeated, tumbling across the path.

"Follow them, I said!" Nussler screamed with such intensity that all the birds flew out of the trees. Just as the machine approached the fallen branch, it began to turn, lurching to one side. But its wheel caught in a deep rut, sending WC Squirrel to the ground. From behind the branch, another girl, with blonde hair, blue eyes, and glasses, jumped out and pulled WC away from the path of Nussler's machine just as it was about to run over him.

"Sir!" called one of the squirrels steering the machine. "Do you want us to go back?"

"No!" Nussler shrieked. "Never mind him! We can deal with him later. We must continue! Faster!"

The machine struggled with its left front wheel caught in the rut. It shook from side to side and Nussler could barely keep himself steady.

"Clem!" the blonde girl yelled behind them. "Keep an eye on our friends. Carter! Come with me!"

With that, the blonde girl grabbed a small box from a satchel on the ground. Then she and a young man dashed past the machine. As it began to turn, both wheels on the left side fell into the rut, pitching it sideways and nearly tipping over. While the machine struggled to stay upright, the two humans raced down the path, toward the other two girls.

Nussler slammed his fist into the top of the machine. "After them!" he screamed, pounding his fist harder to punctuate every word. "Get this thing moving!"

As the driver tried to maneuver out of the rut, Nussler watched the humans run up the path and catch up to the cartwheeling girls. He could see all his plans slipping through his fingers, proving that he was still an embarrassing failure.

"NOW!" he screamed, his bulging eyes wild with rage. "We must not fail!"

A stray tuft of fur tumbled over Nussler's forehead as the driver managed to pull the machine up and out of the rut. He slicked his fur back into place on his head. The machine sputtered momentarily, then lurched forward.

"Get up the path!" he yelled.

The three girls and the young man had reached the stream now. Gathering rocks and loose branches, they began piling them into the stream. As the machine approached, a trickle of water began to run down the path.

The driver slowed the machine at the sight of the water.

"What are you doing?" Nussler shouted. "Don't slow down!"

"The water," the driver called out. "We'll need to avoid it when it starts turning the path to mud."

"I was very clear in my instructions to Otto and the Superior Squirrels that this machine was to be built to cover all terrain! That includes mud!" Nussler yelled. "You will continue on this path or suffer the consequences. That is an order!"

"That is an order!" repeated Otto and his group of Superior Squirrels, who had now taken their position behind the machine.

Finally. Just like Otto to show up late. Imbecile.

The driver floored the accelerator, gaining traction and powering forward. As the machine plowed up the path, the trickle of water slowly became a thin but steady flow. Nussler felt the machine shift and jostle, slipping on the wet earth.

"We're too heavy," the driver yelled. "We need to offload some weight."

With that, Nussler turned and motioned for two of the Superior Squirrels to approach the machine. "Dump some of those branches," he commanded.

"Sir," Otto said, "won't we be needing those?"

Nussler reached back and grabbed Otto by the throat, yanking him off the ground. "Do not question me," he snarled. "We will make this work. It is our destiny."

He dropped Otto to the ground with a thud. Gagging and choking, Otto tumbled a few feet down the path. When he got up to straighten himself out, he doubled over and clutched his ribs. Wheezing, he hung back and watched.

"You coward!" Nussler shouted. "I knew I couldn't trust you!"

Running along either side of Nussler, the two Superior Squirrels did as they were told, awkwardly reaching over to grab the stacked branches and tossing them away. They struggled to keep up with the machine, which was now accelerating at a more even rate with each branch unloaded.

"Faster!" Nussler screamed again. "Victory will be ours!"

The water was running faster now and spreading out along the entire path. Below the machine's wheels, the dirt was turning into mud, slowing their pace.

"We are almost there," Nussler said as they approached the bank of the stream. The Great White Oak was just a short distance to the east. Nussler felt its white glow on his face, and he soaked up its pure, unsullied power as he gave his orders. "Do not let up!"

Just then, the blonde girl reached into the box. She slipped on a pair of gloves and then pulled out an odd blue object. Nussler squinted, trying to make out the shape. If he didn't know any better, he would've thought it was an icicle. *But how could that be? No one could keep an icicle inside a box.*

The girl held up the blue object as the others gathered behind her. They were nearly within striking distance now, mere feet away from the sputtering machine coming up the embankment.

"Nussler!" she yelled. "You are an evil tyrant with sick, twisted ideas. You will torment these innocent gray squirrels no longer."

"You're just a girl. What can you possibly know about me?"

"I know enough," the girl said defiantly. "And I know something you don't."

"Oh?" he toyed with her as the machine rumbled closer. "And what is that?"

She set her jaw and stood tall. "It's going to be extremely hot where you're going. So, let me take this opportunity to cool you off before you go."

"*Where I'm going?*" he asked with a condescending laugh. "What does *that* mean?"

But before she could answer, she plunged the blue object against the water diverted onto the path. As soon as it made contact, the streaming water froze solid. The machine spun out on the ice and began to skid backwards down the path.

"NO!" Nussler screamed, slipping and sliding along the roof. "Get this under control!"

But the machine continued to fall backwards, mowing over the Superior Squirrels. Nussler felt each one roll under the machine's wheels with a bump more forceful than the last. Finally, the machine skidded sideways, tossing Nussler from the roof. He landed directly behind the rear wheels and heard the driver try to power it back up the hill. Then with a mighty burst of momentum, it crushed Nussler, pinning him to the ground and halting momentarily. He gurgled and slapped at the icy ground, trying to get to his feet. Without warning, the machine started moving again. In a failed attempt to propel forward, it spun out of control, gaining altitude. Then it sailed through the air, smashing into the base of the Great White Oak. As the remnants of the destroyed machine came to rest, a deafening crack echoed through the forest.

From his back, Nussler could only watch as the Great White Oak disintegrated. He was helpless now, unable to move or speak. Gasping for breath, he saw a thick portion of its mighty trunk shoot through the air. It was the last thing he saw before it landed on his chest, crushing him.

CHAPTER EIGHT

Snowy looked up from the ground, still reverberating from the explosion. Carter had thrown himself over her, Minty, and Goldie. As she pulled herself up, her vision came into focus. Eyes wide, she quickly jerked her head away, sickened by the sight and sound of Nussler being crushed to death. Instead, she fixed on the Great White Oak, or at least the spot where it had stood until moments ago. All that remained was a few scattered branches, nearly everything else reduced to twigs or less. A shower of splintering white fragments cascaded down, coating everything with a fine powder.

The machine's dazed driver staggered from its destroyed hull. Otto came up to him, with WC Squirrel a step behind. As Otto lifted one of the driver's arms, WC took the other. Together, they helped the driver sit down on a nearby boulder so he could catch his breath. Otto and WC stood, then faced each other.

Snowy got to her feet while Carter helped Minty and Goldie.

"Everyone alright?" Snowy asked.

They all nodded and dusted themselves off, then walked over to the clearing where WC and Otto stood. Goldie coughed from inhaling the falling ash as Minty carried her. Clem was standing by the large fallen branch. Little by little, groups of gray squirrels began emerging from the hole that had been dug behind the fallen tree branch.

"WC," Snowy said as they approached, "it's so good to see you."

"Oh, my dear Miss Snowy, I should say it is so good to see *you*," WC replied. "I was afraid I wasn't going to make it. The gray squirrels and I owe you everything. Thank you for your brave actions."

"I didn't do it alone," Snowy said, laying a hand on Minty's shoulder. "My best friend Minty, and our friends Goldie and Carter, helped. And that's Clem over there."

WC bowed to them in appreciation. "My sincerest gratitude to all of you," he said.

By now, the ground was swarming with gray squirrels, cautiously surfacing from their hiding place. Slowly, brown squirrels began to make their way toward the group, respectfully keeping their distance.

"It was our pleasure," Minty answered, giving Snowy a smile. "I'm glad we were able to help."

"We have been at odds with the brown squirrels for so long," WC said, "and I was about to give up hope. We will be eternally grateful for your assistance. But we are not quite finished here."

With that, WC turned to Otto and the two of them studied each other momentarily. With the brown and gray squirrels now assembled, he surveyed the scene before him. Wiping the white dust from his fur, WC began, "Nussler was an awful tyrant and to be honest, I'm glad he has met his end. His ideas of supremacy and inferiority are dangerous and must not be allowed to infiltrate any aspect of society again."

Otto, sweating and coughing softly from the still settling ash, nodded his head. His eyes were empty, defeated. "I ... I must agree," he uttered quietly. "To be honest, I am relieved to be out from under his control."

A soft murmur echoed through the crowd of gray and brown squirrels.

"I suspected you might be," WC said. "And if that's the case, I would like to ask for your surrender to the gray squirrels. With one condition."

Otto's eyes widened. "Condition?"

WC's face slowly broke into a wide grin. "There is still a peace treaty to be signed," he reminded. "If you will sign it, we can all agree to live in peace, brown and gray squirrels, side by side, from this moment forward."

Otto's lips slowly morphed into a smile. "That would be most agreeable," he said.

They exchanged a hearty paw-shake and slapped each other on the back as all the squirrels erupted in joyful chatter. "Come on," WC said, "let's do it."

Withing moments, the treaty was signed followed by more paw-shakes. Snowy clapped her hands in delight.

"This is wonderful," she said. "I'm so happy for all of you. And now, we can be on our way home."

"Oh, Miss Snowy, I must insist on giving you a gift before you go," WC said.

"A gift?" she asked, bewildered. "That's not necessary."

"Rubbish," WC replied. "Something tells me you'll be needing this very special item. Now, will all of you please follow me?"

He walked to the back of the Great White Oak's stump and picked up a large, gleaming branch, seemingly unaffected by the explosion. With another bow, he presented it to Snowy.

"I give you The Scepter of the Trees," he proclaimed. "You'll be needing it when you get back to England. And I promise, it won't be long now before you're in Epping Forest."

"Epping Forest?" Snowy gasped with surprise. "How do you know?"

WC nodded. "That's a secret," he said. "Now, if I were you, I'd hurry back to that ship of yours. Seems like we have a storm rolling in."

Snowy looked up at the sky, framed by the tall trees of the forest. It was bright blue as far as she could see. She looked at WC, who merely nodded.

"Don't wait," he said. "Go on."

They all shook hands and turned to depart.

"Can I carry the scepter?" Goldie asked.

"It might be too heavy for you," Snowy said.

"Oh no," WC chimed in. "I think it'll be just right."

Goldie took the scepter and held it aloft, then pointed it toward the direction of the farmer's field. "To Epping!" she called. Clem scooped her up and put her on his shoulders. With the scepter hoisted, she led the way through the forest. She coughed now and then.

"Are you not feeling well?" Clem asked her.

"I think it's all the dust," Goldie said.

"When we get back to the ship, let's get you a drink from the pitcher that Lyr and the Okeanos gave us," Snowy advised. "That will give you some fresh water. In fact, we should all have some."

As they got to the edge of the forest, Snowy saw the crew, all standing around the ship.

"What's this?" Snowy asked as they came up to the ship.

"Storm's coming in," Rogers said.

Again, Snowy looked up, seeing nothing but blue sky.

"So, what are you doing out here?" she asked, confused.

"Just getting ready to pray," he said. "Please join us."

Snowy and Minty looked at each other, and Minty gave her a wink. Snowy, Minty, Goldie, Carter, and Clem found a place in the circle of crew members gathered around the ship. Goldie fiddled with the scepter.

"Ooh," she squealed, eyes fixed on the scepter. "Look at this!"

"Not now," Minty said, "we're going to say prayers first."

Everyone moved in close to the *G2* and joined hands.

"Clem," Snowy said, "would you like to lead us?"

"Of course," he said.

As he bowed his head, everyone put one hand on the side of the ship. They bowed their heads and closed their eyes, waiting for his prayer. Except Goldie, who held the gleaming white scepter.

"Let me see that," Minty whispered, motioning for Goldie to give it to her.

Reluctantly, Goldie passed it to Minty. And when she did, Minty accidentally bumped the scepter against Carter's shoulder. Regaining her grip, she ran a finger over a small knot on the branch. As she touched it, a crack of thunder erupted. Snowy jumped at the noise.

But when she opened her eyes, she couldn't believe what she saw. The *G2*, along with the crew, had landed on the grass, right outside her cottage in Epping Forest. She looked around, mystified. There was the cottage, the meadow, the path that led to Minty's house, the observatory on the top floor, the warm sunlight streaming on her face. Claudette was sweeping the porch while Annelise and Camille played in the grass with another girl.

"Goldie!" Snowy exclaimed, surprised to see her little friend on the grass.

"What?" asked Goldie with a giggle, standing behind Snowy.

Snowy turned and looked at Goldie, and then back to the three girls playing on the lawn. The resemblance was undeniable. Snowy shook her head as she looked back at the girls. They were in front of a rose bush, laughing and giggling together.

"I don't remember that rose bush being there before," Snowy said, still confused about the new girl playing with Claudette's daughters. "When did that spring up?"

Claudette clasped her hand over her mouth and stopped sweeping, no doubt shocked at the sight of a ship landing in front of the cottage. Snowy smiled and then closed her eyes, unable to take it all in. It had been a long journey, and she could learn more about the rose bush and the mysterious little girl later. For now, at last, she was home.

About the Author

Justin Mitson lives in Garden City, Idaho. A technologist and entrepreneur, he loves to write fun, engaging stories, from children's adventures and mob comedies to deep science fiction and time travel tales. Born in Butte, Montana, he spent most of his childhood roaming around the northwest, living in eighteen different locations before getting through high school. This gave him a sense of adventure and encouraged his imagination. A student of history as well as technology, Mr. Channing loves to ask, "what if?" When he's not writing, he's an avid water ski and snow ski enthusiast (and occasionally does those two activities on the same day) and loves to ride his electronic skateboard on the miles of the Boise area's greenbelt. Above all, his greatest joy is making his wife and two daughters laugh.